BBC
DOCTOR WHO

A HISTORY
OF HUMANKIND

The Doctor's
OFFICIAL
Guide

BBC CHILDREN'S BOOKS

UK | USA | Canada | Ireland | Australia | India | New Zealand | South Africa

BBC Children's Books are published by Puffin Books, part of the Penguin Random House group of
companies whose addresses can be found at global.penguinrandomhouse.com
www.penguin.co.uk   www.puffin.co.uk   www.ladybird.co.uk

Penguin
Random House
UK

First published by Puffin Books 2016
001

Written by Justin Richards
Illustrations by Dan Green
Copyright © BBC Worldwide Limited, 2016
BBC, DOCTOR WHO (word marks, logos and devices), TARDIS, DALEKS, CYBERMAN and K-9
(word marks and devices) are trademarks of the British Broadcasting Corporation
and are used under licence.
BBC logo © BBC, 1996. Doctor Who logo © BBC, 2009

DOCTOR WHO

A HISTORY
OF HUMANKIND

The Doctor's
OFFICIAL
Guide

CONTENTS

BORING
BORING
BORING!!!
WHO READS THE
CONTENTS PAGE
ANYWAY?!
JUST TURN OVER!

INTRODUCTION

THERE WAS ANOTHER INTRODUCTION HERE, BUT IT WAS RUBBISH SO I'VE STUCK THIS HERE TO SAVE YOU HAVING TO READ IT.

UTTER DRIVEL.

HONESTLY.

I mean, yes, history is important - very important - but you don't have to be so pompous about it. Especially as a lot of the history in this book was just wrong.

But it's all right – I've fixed
it. I've taken out the rubbish,
useless, inaccurate stuff and
added more interesting
accounts of what
really happened.
I hope you enjoy it – but even
if you don't, at least you'll be
learning something useful.

NOTE TO THE COAL HILL
SCHOOL LIBRARIAN

I don't know how you decide which books to
buy for the library, but this one is a real
stinker. You're lucky I found it and sorted
it out. Maybe in future you should consult
me before purchasing.

~~The Doctor~~ John Smith,
caretaker (sometimes)

Oh, and I'm looking at the science
section next – you have been warned!

PREHISTORY
The Start of Life on Earth

HOW LIFE BEGAN on our planet is still something of a mystery. Some scientists think that life appeared as soon as the Earth's environment was stable enough to support it. The Earth is about 4.5 billion years old, but the earliest fossilised bacteria that have been found date back only 3.4 billion years.

NO IT ISN'T.

WHICH IS ANOTHER WAY OF SAYING YOU DON'T KNOW.

There are several theories as to how life started. Some say micro-organisms arrived from outer space, perhaps via a comet. Others believe that life started in several different ways in different places.

JAGAROTH SPACESHIP

Life began on Earth because of the Jagaroth. Nasty, callous, warlike lot, the Jagaroth. The last of them crash-landed on Earth and tried to take off again, but their atmospheric thrust motors were broken so they used their spaceship's warp drive . . . and it exploded.

The explosion sparked the first life in the amniotic fluid below. Amino acids fused into cells, which eventually evolved into plant and animal life.

BOOM.

It was a bit more complicated than that, though, because a Jagaroth called Scaroth got splintered through time and tried to go back and stop the explosion. Lucky I was there, really, or else there'd be no human race.

SCAROTH

THE AGE OF THE DINOSAURS

DINOSAURS WERE just one form of prehistoric life. They lived on Earth for around 165 million years before they became extinct. The word dinosaur comes from the term *Dinosauria* (meaning 'terrible lizard'), which was coined by English scientist Sir Richard Owen in 1842, although dinosaur bones and fossils had been found as early as 1818.

ONLY BECAUSE I SUGGESTED IT TO HIM.

There was no intelligent life on Earth at the time of the dinosaurs, and humans did not evolve until millions of years later. ← **WHAT?! WHO WROTE THIS DRIVEL?????**

No intelligent life? What about Homo reptilia, or the Silurians as they've also been called? They had a whole civilisation when humankind were just apes!

THE VARIOUS TYPES OF SILURIANS I'VE MET.

But then the Silurians detected a small planet drifting through space — they thought it would collide with Earth and wipe out all life, so some of them left in spaceships, and most went into hibernation deep underground. They're still there, because the small planet never hit. It went into orbit and became the Moon. No collision, no catastrophe. Nothing to wake the Silurians up.

DINOSAUR EXTINCTION

There were a couple of pages here giving all sorts of daft theories about why the dinosaurs became extinct - stuff about meteors and asteroids and comets. All complete rubbish.

Look, it's all quite simple. The dinosaurs were wiped out when a space freighter drifted back in time because it was fitted with Cyber technology. The Cybermen were trying to destroy a peace conference on Earth in the future, but I got involved and it all went a bit wrong for them. The freighter crashed into Earth 65 million years ago and its antimatter containment vessel split open. Huge explosion. End of the dinosaurs.

And the end of my friend Adric too, sadly, as he was on board.

Anyway, you're humans — don't you remember that London was evacuated because dinosaurs appeared? That was only about, what, forty years ago in your timestream? That's almost yesterday.

OK, so the dinosaurs were brought forward in time by Professor Whitaker with a timescoop as part of his insane Operation Golden Age project, but even so. It happened. I was there. And I put a stop to it. As usual.

A DEVICE THAT SCOOPS THINGS UP FROM ONE TIME AND DUMPS THEM IN ANOTHER TIME — HENCE THE NAME, SEE?

THE STONE AGE

THEY WERE PRETTY HANDY WITH A STONE, PREHISTORIC HUMANS. REMARKABLE, REALLY.

HUMAN PREHISTORY is divided into three periods based on the technology used by humankind at the time. These are, in order, the Stone Age, the Bronze Age, and the Iron Age.

In the Stone Age, humans began to fashion and use tools. Some tools were made with a point, others with a sharp edge for cutting. *THEY DID A LOT OF BASHING OF THINGS TOO, I SEEM TO REMEMBER*

It was also during the Stone Age that the human race discovered fire and how to control it.

IS THAT ALL YOU'RE GOING TO SAY ABOUT FIRE? FIRE WAS HUGE. FIRE WAS THE BIGGIE.

I met one tribe who had lost the secret of fire, and they were not a happy bunch, I can tell you. They'd cave your head in if they didn't like you – another use for a stone-bashing tool. Kept the skulls as trophies.

Or maybe as warnings.

To be honest, I didn't ask. Didn't hang about either. I set fire to some stuff, which got their attention, then scarpered.

STONEHENGE

I SEE YOU'RE BEING AS EXACT AS EVER

STONEHENGE IS ONE of the most famous prehistoric sites in the world. Located in Wiltshire, England, it is thought to have been constructed between 3000 BC and 2000 BC. The main site consists of a ring of standing stones, though many are now missing or have fallen down.

There is some debate about how the huge stones were transported to the site and erected there. The purpose of Stonehenge is also one of the mysteries of the ancient world. It may have been constructed as an observatory or as a religious site.

THE MEDDLING MONK TOLD ME HE USED AN ANTI-GRAVITATIONAL LIFT.

Not going to mention the Underhenge, then? That's the huge cavern beneath Stonehenge where an alliance of all sorts of alien life forms kept the Pandorica, and where I very nearly came to a rather sticky end. Not nice, all those alien life forms just suddenly deciding that it must have been my fault that the universe was about to end.

Well, maybe it was my fault, but even so.

I sorted it out, though. Rebooted the universe and put everything back together so it was just as good as before. If 'good' is the right word. Sometimes I'm not sure.

ANCIENT EGYPT AND THE PYRAMIDS

ONLY ONE of the Seven Wonders of the Ancient World is still intact today: the Great Pyramid of Giza in Egypt. It stands over 140 metres tall and took twenty years to build. The pyramids were built as grand tombs for the pharaohs, who were the rulers of Egypt. The pyramids date back to the times of the so-called Old Kingdom and Middle Kingdom.

DOESN'T ANYONE USE DATES ANY MORE? DATES ARE USEFUL. THOUGH OF COURSE THEY DIDN'T KNOW WHAT YEAR BC IT WAS AT THE TIME . . .

Scaroth, the last of the Jagaroth, would tell you he had quite a lot to do with building the pyramids. Which would explain a lot, because historians can never make up their minds about how the pyramids were actually built. That said, Scaroth was rather full of himself, so it could all be wild exaggeration. And you can do a lot with thousands of slaves (but that's no excuse for having them).

I was there briefly when they were building the Great Pyramid. Didn't see Scaroth – and he's quite distinctive, what with his green skin and one eye. But then I was busy trying to stop the Daleks from getting hold of the core of their Time Destructor, which I'd stolen. One thing I learned: ancient Egyptians and Daleks don't get on.

THE ANCIENT EGYPTIAN GODS

THE PEOPLE OF ANCIENT EGYPT believed in many different gods and goddesses. The gods oversaw all aspects of ancient Egyptian life and death. They were the ancient Egyptians' way of explaining the world in which they lived.

Exactly how many gods and goddesses the ancient Egyptians worshipped is difficult to assess, but it was certainly over 1,500 and possibly as many as 2,000.

THERE WERE 740. PLUS SUTEKH. THE REST ARE MADE UP.

It's all based on the Osirans,
one of whom, Sutekh, was a
particularly unpleasant character.
Believe me, I met him. Not nice.
He even destroyed his own world,
Phaester Osiris, then left a
trail of devastation across half
the galaxy. The other Osirans,
led by Horus, finally caught up
with him in ancient Egypt.
I doubt that was much
fun for anyone, but
the wars of the
gods entered into
Egyptian mythology.

They imprisoned Sutekh beneath a pyramid and just left him
there to rot, or whatever Osirans do. He didn't manage to
escape until 1911 – so I guess he did lots of sitting around
and getting bored. When he did escape, I was there. Luckily.
So I had to save the planet, and quite possibly the whole galaxy.

AGAIN.

LIFE IN ANCIENT EGYPT

THE WIFE of Pharoah Akhenaten was Nefertiti, who some believe ruled on her own after his death. Together they had six daughters.

NOT SURE THE PICTURE DOES HER JUSTICE. OK, SHE DID LOOK A BIT LIKE THAT, BUT IT DOESN'T REALLY SHOW HOW BRILLIANT AND FEISTY SHE WAS.

The period under the rule of Akhenaten and Nefertiti was perhaps the wealthiest period of ancient Egyptian history. Strangely, no burial place for Nefertiti has been identified, and her mummy has never been found.

NOT THAT STRANGE GIVEN THAT SHE DIED IN THE MIDDLE OF THE TWENTIETH CENTURY.

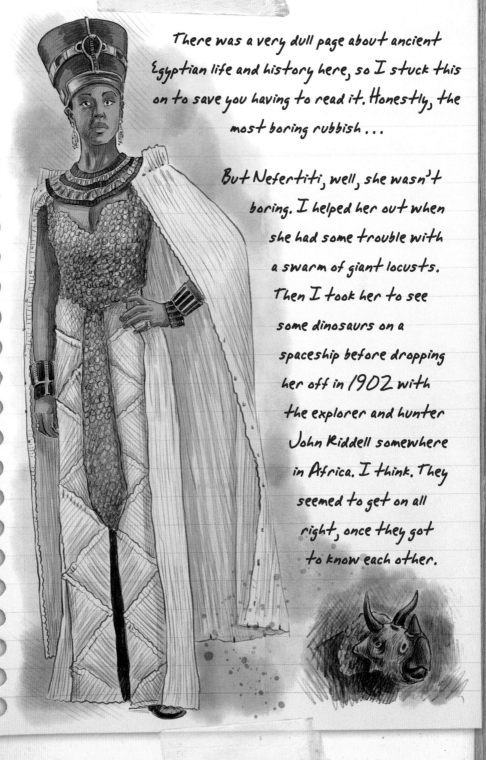

There was a very dull page about ancient Egyptian life and history here, so I stuck this on to save you having to read it. Honestly, the most boring rubbish...

But Nefertiti, well, she wasn't boring. I helped her out when she had some trouble with a swarm of giant locusts. Then I took her to see some dinosaurs on a spaceship before dropping her off in 1902 with the explorer and hunter John Riddell somewhere in Africa. I think. They seemed to get on all right, once they got to know each other.

THE LEGEND OF ATLANTIS

← NO.

ATLANTIS IS A FICTIONAL island first mentioned by the Greek philosopher Plato. The legend goes that Atlantis was located 'beyond the Pillars of Hercules' and went to war with Athens. It fell out of favour with the gods, and sank beneath the waves.

↖ WELL, THAT MUCH IS TRUE. NOT THE GODS BIT, BUT THE SINKING.

I DON'T KNOW WHERE TO START WITH THIS ONE. ATLANTIS EXISTED. END OF.

In fact, it may have existed several times. The Dæmons claimed to have destroyed it, but that might just have been bluster – they're full of bluster, the Dæmons.

Anyway, Atlantis certainly sank. It got flooded when Professor Zaroff tried to drain the oceans into the Earth's core. He was a complete loony and then some. Crazy as a nutty fruitcake. Bonkers bananas.

I went to Atlantis a long time before that, too, during the reign of King Dalios. The Master tried to steal the throne so he could get control of Kronos the Chronovore. Long story. Didn't end well ...

THE MYTH OF THE MINOTAUR

IN GREEK MYTH, the Minotaur is a creature with the body of a man and the head of a bull. It was imprisoned by King Minos of Crete in the middle of a huge, specially designed maze built at Knossos, which was called the Labyrinth.

Forced to pay tribute to Minos, Athens sent seven young men and seven young women every nine years to be devoured by the Minotaur. The Athenian prince Theseus insisted on going as one of the men, and – helped by Ariadne, the daughter of King Minos – he slew the Minotaur.

Ariadne gave Theseus a big ball of thread so he could mark his route and find his way out of the Labyrinth again. And I gave Ariadne the thread. If I hadn't, she and Theseus were going to unravel my scarf – the cheek of it!

But, actually, creatures with heads like bulls aren't that uncommon. There's the Nimon – nasty scavengers. Had a run-in with them once. Not a pleasant lot. I also came across another Minotaur-like creature that was a sort of cousin of the Nimon. They turned up on primitive worlds, made out that they were gods, and then fed on the people's faith. Not nice, basically.

THE SIEGE OF TROY

ACCORDING TO LEGEND, the Greeks besieged the ancient city of Troy for ten years before they finally devised a plan to take the city. They constructed a huge wooden horse – an animal sacred to the Trojans. The horse was hollow, and some of the Greek soldiers hid inside while the others sailed away. As the Greeks had hoped, the Trojans dragged the enormous wooden horse into their walled city. That night, the soldiers hidden inside the horse attacked the sleeping Trojans and opened the city gates to their returning army.

I'M SORRY – WHO DEVISED THE PLAN?

IT WAS ALL MY IDEA.

Under duress, I might add. I was captured by Odysseus. I pretended to be Zeus, king of the gods, but they weren't quite as impressed as I'd hoped. They gave me two days to come up with a plan to take the city of Troy.

I always thought the wooden horse was a daft idea, actually, so I made a few other suggestions first. Flying machines that could be catapulted over the city walls with soldiers strapped to them, for example. Odysseus quite liked that one. But he insisted on me being the first to try it out, and it suddenly didn't seem like quite such a good idea after all.

So wooden horse it was, no matter how improbable.

29

THE ROMAN EMPIRE

AT ITS HEIGHT, the Roman Empire was the most extensive political and social structure in the Western world.

The empire survived various attacks and setbacks, including the Great Fire of Rome in 64 AD. This devastated the city and took six days to be brought under control. While Emperor Nero blamed the fire on the Christians, some historians suggest that he may have started the fire himself.

LIKE HAVING THOUSANDS OF SOLDIERS KIDNAPPED BY ALIENS AND MADE TO FIGHT IN THEIR WAR GAMES.

WELL, OF COURSE HE DID.

And here's what actually happened:

NERO WANTED TO REBUILD ROME (AND NAME IT AFTER HIMSELF – TALK ABOUT ARROGANT).

THE SENATE WOULDN'T AGREE, SO HE WAS A BIT STUCK.

SOMEONE ACCIDENTALLY SET FIRE TO NERO'S PLANS FOR THE NEW CITY. (I WON'T SAY WHO, BECAUSE THAT'S JUST A TEENY-WEENY BIT EMBARRASSING.)

THIS GAVE NERO THE IDEA TO BURN DOWN THE REAL CITY TO MAKE WAY FOR HIS NEW ONE.

THEN HE BLAMED THE CHRISTIANS. NOT SURE WHY THEY'D WANT TO BURN DOWN ROME, BUT THERE YOU GO.

Can't say I took to Nero, really. I did convince him I was a terrific lyre player, but his response was to try to have me play in the arena while being attacked by lions and alligators. I don't think he really appreciated talent.

POMPEII AND THE ERUPTION OF VESUVIUS

MOUNT VESUVIUS, on the west coast of Italy, is one of the only volcanoes in mainland Europe to have erupted in the last 100 years. But it is most famous for its eruption back in 79 AD, when it caused huge devastation.

YOU'RE TELLING M

When Vesuvius erupted, the nearby city of Pompeii was still recovering from the effects of an earthquake that had struck in 62 AD. Pompeii, the neighbouring town of Herculaneum, and several other local Roman settlements were buried in ash. It is not known how many died in the disaster, but about 1,500 bodies have been unearthed in Pompeii and Herculaneum.

It was my fault, I'm afraid. Well, I was only putting history back on track. The Pyroviles were going to use the energy from Mount Vesuvius to set up a fusion matrix and turn everyone on Earth into Pyroviles. There wouldn't have been an eruption, but then there also wouldn't have been a human race. So I didn't have much of a choice, really.

THE LEGACY OF POMPEII

NOT A LOT OF CONSOLATION FOR THE PEOPLE WHO DIED, THOUGH.

Preserved under volcanic ash, Pompeii now provides a unique record of life in a Roman city. Not only have archaeologists been able to unearth buildings, but also many of the contents of these buildings. The bits and pieces of everyday life have been preserved, including utensils, furniture, ornaments, lamps and even some foodstuffs. Many paintings have also survived, as have the bodies of victims buried in the eruption.

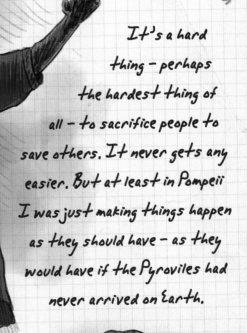

It's a hard thing – perhaps the hardest thing of all – to sacrifice people to save others. It never gets any easier. But at least in Pompeii I was just making things happen as they should have – as they would have if the Pyroviles had never arrived on Earth.

And I did save someone. Donna made me go back, and I'm glad she did, because I saved Caecilius and his family. That's what I do, when I can: I save people. And, to make sure I never forget that, I now wear Caecilius's face. The eyebrows took some getting used to, though . . .

THE VIKINGS

THEY CERTAINLY GOT ABOUT. THEY STUCK ME AND CLARA ON A BOAT FOR TWO DAYS. TWO DAYS!

FROM THEIR HOMES IN SCANDINAVIA, the Vikings raided – and traded with – large areas of northern and central Europe from the late eighth to late eleventh centuries. Advanced seafarers as well as warriors, the Vikings also explored and colonised, reaching as far as Iceland, Greenland and even Canada.

I PRETENDED TO BE ODIN ONCE. DIDN'T WORK OUT THAT WELL BECAUSE ANOTHER IMPOSTER TURNED UP WITH BETTER TECHNOLOGY. I HAD A YO-YO; HE MADE HIS FACE APPEAR IN THE SKY.

Like the ancient Greeks and Romans, the Vikings worshipped many gods and goddesses. Their three most important gods were: Odin, the god of war, poetry and death; Freyr, the god of agriculture and fertility; and Thor, the god of thunder, who also protected the Vikings from cold, hunger, giants and other dangers.

The Vikings weren't all warriors. Some were, yes – but, when you've had to try to train a few Viking farmers and blacksmiths to use swords without chopping off their own fingers, you get to know who's a warrior and who isn't.

They thought Odin had turned up, but the imposter was one of the Mire – even nastier and more warlike than the Vikings. Took a lot of clever thinking to see him and his warriors off, I can tell you, and it cost a poor young girl called Ashildr her life. But I managed to resurrect her – I made her pretty much immortal.

I'M STILL NOT SURE WHETHER THAT WAS THE RIGHT THING TO DO.

THE NORMAN CONQUEST OF ENGLAND

There was a rather complicated explanation of events here, so I've made it better. Here's what happened:

AT THE BEGINNING OF THE YEAR 1066, KING EDWARD THE CONFESSOR DIED CHILDLESS. VERY SAD.

SO IN JANUARY OF THAT SAME YEAR, HIS BROTHER-IN-LAW HAROLD GODWINSON BECAME KING.

IN SEPTEMBER, THE NORWEGIAN KING HARALD HARDRADA INVADED NORTHERN ENGLAND.

KING HAROLD MARCHED NORTH ASAP AND DEFEATED HARDRADA.

BUT THEN WILLIAM OF NORMANDY (AKA WILLIAM THE CONQUEROR) INVADED SOUTHERN ENGLAND.

HAROLD HAD TO MARCH SOUTH AGAIN.

> HIS ARMY WAS PRETTY TIRED FROM ALL THAT MARCHING.

> HAROLD WAS DEFEATED BY WILLIAM AT THE BATTLE OF HASTINGS – THOUGH IT WASN'T ACTUALLY AT HASTINGS, BUT THAT'S ANOTHER STORY.

I've never been to the Battle of Hastings. I really must go along one day and take a look.

I have been to Britain in 1066, but further north. Met another Time Lord there disguised as a monk. He had this daft plan to destroy Harald Hardrada's fleet when it arrived so that King Harold would have a fresh army (instead of one that had marched up and down so much) and would win the Battle of Hastings.

I'm not quite sure what the Monk hoped to achieve. He seemed to think that Harold was a better king than William would be, but that's hardly a justification for messing about with history like that.

RICHARD THE LIONHEART

RICHARD I OF ENGLAND reigned from 1189 until his death in 1199. He is known as Richard the Lionheart because of his reputation as a great military leader and soldier. *HE HAD QUITE A TEMPER TOO.*

Although he was King of England, he actually spent very little time in the country, and was one of the main Christian leaders of the Third Crusade of 1189 to 1192. These leaders aimed to retake Jerusalem from the Muslims led by Saladin, although they were ultimately unsuccessful.

When I met him during the crusade, Richard was in the city of Jaffa. He'd got a bit tired of all the fighting, to be honest. Wanted to broker peace by marrying off his sister Joanna to Saladin's brother Saphadin. Trouble was, Joanna wasn't that keen.

Richard wasn't too happy either. He thought that I'd told his sister what he was planning, but actually that wasn't me at all. He got a bit friendlier when he found that out. And he knighted my friend Ian Chesterton, which was good of him. Didn't offer me a knighthood, though.

THE LEGEND OF ROBIN HOOD

THE LEGEND OF Robin Hood has endured for centuries. The courageous twelfth-century outlaw of English folklore was an expert archer and swordsman who lived in Sherwood Forest with his band of Merry Men. He is said to have robbed from the rich and given the proceeds to the poor, while being hunted by the Sheriff of Nottingham.

Expert swordsman? I saw him off with a spoon.

HE DIDN'T LOOK ANYTHING LIKE THAT. THE HAIR'S ALL WRONG FOR A START. AND HE WASN'T COURAGEOUS; HE WAS ARROGANT. AND BEARDY.

One story tells of how the sheriff held an archery competition with a golden arrow as the prize. The sheriff knew that Robin Hood would enter and win, thereby giving the sheriff an opportunity to identify the infamous outlaw and have him arrested.

Merry Men? Merry isn't the half of it. Banter, banter, banter, all day long. It's surprising they got any outlaw stuff done at all.

Talking of which, I didn't see any evidence of giving to the poor — or robbing from the rich, come to that. It was all a bit cosy and smug.

And that archery competition? An obvious trap, for one thing. And, for another, Robin didn't win it. I did. Well technically I cheated. If you count blowing up the target as cheating.

Academics and historians tend to agree that the legend of Robin Hood must be based, at least in part, on an actual person from history. If Robin Hood did exist, it has been suggested that he might have been the Earl of Huntingdon.

NOT SURPRISING SINCE HE WAS AN ACTUAL PERSON FROM HISTORY.

IT PAINS ME TO ADMIT IT, BUT HE DID. YES, SURPRISED ME TOO, BUT THERE YOU GO.

Nottingham ~~Castle~~

SPACESHIP

Funny how stories and legends grow up around someone, isn't it? I mean, I've met Robin Hood and I'm still not sure who or what he really was. He just wasn't a very convincing real person. All that banter - it's not natural.

Maybe he was a robot - like the Sheriff of Nottingham and his knights turned out to be. Not Robin of Sherwood, but Robot of Sherwood. It's possible. Well, OK, it's unlikely, but then so is rice pudding.

And I suppose I can see some value in a man born into privilege deciding to leave the comfort of his home to go out into the universe and help the weak and oppressed. Yes, that has a ring of truth about it.

KING JOHN AND MAGNA CARTA

THE YOUNGEST OF HENRY II'S SONS, John, became King of England after the death of his brother Richard the Lionheart in 1199. John is not remembered as a good king. He is famous for losing the Duchy of Normandy to Philip II of France, and for the revolt of the barons, which led to Magna Carta.

THERE MAY BE A REASON FOR THIS.

Magna Carta was signed at Runnymede in 1215. Magna Carta proposed political reform and covered church rights, protection from illegal imprisonment, access to justice, and taxation.

WHERE WAS MAGNA CARTA SIGNED? AT THE BOTTOM! SORRY – COULDN'T RESIST.

I met King John once.
Or rather, I didn't,
but for a while
I thought I did.

It was at Sir Ranulf Fitzwilliam's castle.
The TARDIS materialised in the middle of a joust,
which attracted a bit of attention - not least
from King John. Who turned out not to be the real
King John. This one was actually a shape-changing
robot called Kamelion, which the Master was using
to try to ensure Magna Carta was never created.
Not quite sure why he wanted to do that...
Just to cause trouble, probably.

MEDIEVAL LIFE

Can't say I ever really took to medieval life, the times I've visited. Not a very pleasant period. Not a very advanced one, either, so I can see why the Meddling Monk brought a few home comforts with him to 1066. Like a record player, and a stove, and a toaster, and a watch. And snuff.

Not sure about snuff, myself. There are enough things in the universe to smell already without sticking more up your nose. Though the medieval period does smell rather different - and not always in a good way.

When I first met Sarah Jane Smith, she sneaked into the TARDIS just as I was setting off for somewhere medieval. She ended up in a castle and thought it was some sort of historical re-enactment. Well, it's an easy mistake.

Still, she turned out to be quite helpful once she understood what was going on. Irongron, the robber baron who owned the castle, was helping a stranded Sontaran to kidnap scientists from the late twentieth century. He wanted them to help repair his damaged spaceship. In return, the Sontaran gave Irongron more modern weapons, and even a fighting robot knight.

He got a bit miffed, though, when he found out the robot was actually me in disguise. Clever, eh?

MARCO POLO

AN ITALIAN MERCHANT TRAVELLER, Marco Polo lived in the late thirteenth and early fourteenth centuries. Although he was not the first European to visit China, he was the first to write a detailed account of his experiences there, and *The Travels of Marco Polo* was published in about 1300.

Returning to Venice after twenty-four years of travelling, Marco Polo found the city at war with Genoa. Marco joined the war, but his ship was captured and he was imprisoned. While in prison, Marco dictated his stories to his cellmate.

WHO EMBELLISHED AND ADDED SOME OF HIS OWN STUFF, I HAVE TO SAY. !!

Marco Polo did travel a lot, but he got quite sick of it. Sometimes I know how he felt. When I met Marco, he just wanted to go home, but he was working for Kublai Khan and couldn't leave without his permission. So he decided to soften the khan up with a gift ... which sounds like a nice idea, except the gift he had in mind was the TARDIS. He took my key and wouldn't let me have it back.

Still, it meant I got to meet Kublai Khan. Nice chap – getting on a bit. We played backgammon. I'm quite good at backgammon. I won thirty-five elephants, 4,000 white stallions, twenty-five tigers, the sacred tooth of Buddha, and all the commerce from Burma for one year.

UNFORTUNATELY, I LOST THE TARDIS.

THE AZTECS

THE AZTEC PEOPLE of Central Mexico dominated the area from the fourteenth to the sixteenth centuries. They worshipped various gods, most notably Huitzilopochtli, the god of war and the sun, to whom human sacrifices were made in which the priest cut out the victim's heart.

The Aztecs often fought 'no-killing' wars. Instead, the opposing armies would take as many prisoners as possible, and the war ended when each side had enough prisoners to sacrifice. *THAT DOESN'T SOUND LIKE 'NO-KILLING' TO ME!*

The Aztecs are also remembered today for their art, jewellery and architecture.

The important thing it doesn't mention anywhere here is cocoa: do NOT make a cup of cocoa for an Aztec. Apparently it counts as a declaration of marriage. No, I didn't know that either, but I found out the hard way. Oh, she was a nice enough lady, called Cameca ... but it would probably never have worked.

They also tried to marry my granddaughter Susan to a sacrificial victim, but she just said no. Sensible girl.

THE RENAISSANCE

THE RENAISSANCE WAS A PERIOD between the fourteenth and the seventeenth centuries when learning and culture in Europe took a great leap forward. Historians consider this period to be the time during which the medieval era transitioned to the modern era.

RATHER DEPENDS ON WHAT YOU MEAN BY 'MODERN'.

It's worth pointing out here that the Renaissance was also a time when the human race was incredibly vulnerable. Suddenly you were showing potential – the potential to progress beyond the confines of your own little planet.

And other life forms were watching – like the Mandragora Helix, which is a spiral of pure energy that no one really understands, not even me. It saw the human race as a potential rival power and tried to kill off most of the great thinkers of the age. Under the influence of the Mandragora Helix, humankind's curiosity wouldn't have stretched beyond the next meal.

So it's lucky I was there to deal with it. Well, maybe not that lucky, since I was the one who brought the Mandragora Helix to Earth in the first place, when some of its energy sneaked into the TARDIS. But it all turned out fine, which is what matters.

LEONARDO DA VINCI

I F THERE IS ONE FIGURE who can be said to exemplify the Renaissance, then it is Leonardo da Vinci. Born in Florence in 1452, Leonardo is best known as a painter. His most famous works include the *Mona Lisa* and *The Last Supper.*

THAT DREADFUL WOMAN WITH NO EYEBROWS WHO WOULDN'T SIT STILL.

Leonardo's interests and talents covered not just art and sculpture, but also architecture, music, mathematics and engineering. He was an inventor whose ideas were often far ahead of their time. ↖

NOT ALL OF THEM WERE VERY PRACTICAL THOUGH. LIKE HIS SUBMARINE – WHAT WAS HE THINKING?

Nice chap, Leonardo. Met him briefly.

I missed him when he was painting the Mona Lisas, though. And no, that's not a mistake – Mona Lisas, plural. Captain Tancredi got him to paint another half-dozen. Tancredi was a splinter of Scaroth the Jagaroth. (Remember him? If not, go back to the prehistory section and try harder.) He wanted lots of copies of the Mona Lisa for a later splinter of himself to sell – he needed money for his time-travel experiments.

The Mona Lisas all got burned – well, all except one, which is now back at the Louvre in Paris. Unfortunately it has THIS IS A FAKE written under the paint in felt pen, but no one's let on about that. I think they were just glad to get it back.

THE MASSACRE OF THE HUGUENOTS

IN AUGUST 1572, Catherine de' Medici, mother of the boy king of France, Charles IX, planned to marry her daughter Margaret to the Protestant prince Henry of Navarre.

OK, COMPLICATED TIMES.
BUT HERE'S WHAT HAPPENED . . .

5 AUGUST 1570: The third of the French Wars of Religion between Catholics and Protestants (Huguenots) ends with the Peace of Saint-Germain-en-Laye. As always, you humans eventually figured out that you were going to have to sit down and talk.

18 AUGUST 1572: Marriage of Henry of Navarre and Margaret of Valois in Paris.

22 AUGUST 1572: Attempted assassination of Huguenot leader Admiral de Coligny. Probably on the orders of Catherine de' Medici (not that you heard it from me).

23 AUGUST 1572: Catherine de' Medici persuades her son King Charles IX to give orders for the Huguenot leaders to be killed.

But things got out of hand, and it became a general massacre of Huguenots, which continued until October. Thousands – possibly tens of thousands – died.

I was there. Well, almost. I got a bit distracted and didn't meet up with my friend Steven Taylor as we'd arranged, which meant Steven went looking for me – and instead found the Abbot of Amboise, who looked uncannily like I used to look back then. It was a bit of a shock to Steven when the Abbot got killed.

Mind you, if he'd just stayed at the tavern like we'd arranged, everything would have been a lot simpler.

That wouldn't have stopped the massacre, though. History can be so very cruel sometimes.

VENICE AND INTERNATIONAL TRADE

AS WELL AS CONTROLLING a huge sea empire, Venice was a major centre of trade and commerce in the Middle Ages. It became a leader in both economic and political affairs within Europe. By the seventeenth century, however, Venice's naval importance was reduced and its trade taken over by other countries such as Portugal.

CIVILISATIONS RISE AND FALL — I'M AFRAID THAT'S HOW HISTORY WORKS, SADLY.

Venice was at its height in 1580 when I was there.
Almost got destroyed.

A Saturnyne called Rosanna
Calvierri (not her real
name) had fled from
her planet when it was
consumed by cracks in
time. She ended up in Venice
with her children - a lot of them,
all sons. So she set up a school to get young Venetian woman
she could convert into brides for her boys.

They're a fishy lot, the
Saturnynes - in every sense.
If I tell you they pretended
to be vampires so that people
wouldn't realise how nasty they
really were, that should give you
some idea. Basically Rosanna was
converting girls into fish, and
planned to sink Venice to create
a nice fishy home for them.

TOLD YOU - FISHY.

QUEEN ELIZABETH I

UM, NOT ACTUALLY TRUE.

Q UEEN ELIZABETH I reigned as Queen of England, Ireland and Wales from 1558 until her death in 1603. She never married so had no children. This meant that she was the last of the Tudor monarchs.

THAT IS TRUE, THOUGH.

The Elizabethan era was noted for seafarers such as Francis Drake and Walter Raleigh. It was during the reign of Elizabeth I that the English defeated the Spanish Armada. Her reign was also notable for the flourishing of drama, with the most famous playwright of the era being, of course, William Shakespeare.

WITH A LOT OF HELP FROM THE WEATHER

You won't find it in any history books – including this one – but Queen Elizabeth was actually married. I know, because she was married to me. She wasn't too happy that I sort of disappeared – dematerialised, you might say – straight after the ceremony. In fact, when she saw me again many years later at the Globe Theatre, she tried to have me executed. I found it all rather confusing as I hadn't actually met her yet, but that's time travel for you.

We got married by accident, really. I only proposed to her because I thought she was a Zygon in disguise. Actually, I'm not sure that makes it sound any better, does it?

WILLIAM SHAKESPEARE

WILLIAM SHAKESPEARE is often described as the world's greatest playwright, and his plays have been translated into every major language. He was born in Stratford-upon-Avon in 1564. Some time after 1585, he moved to London, where he started a career as actor, poet and playwright.

THE LESS SAID ABOUT HIS ACTING ABILITIES, THE BETTER

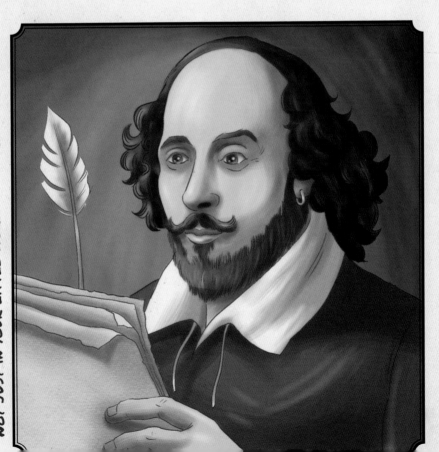

He really was a rubbish actor. I mean awful. Terrible. Pants. 'Stick to the writing,' I told him. But he kept on trying. Never got any better. Good job he was OK with a quill pen – though he did like mixed metaphors, but then no one's perfect.

He liked sonnets too. Sprained his wrist writing too many sonnets, so I had to write for him. He dictated his new play and I wrote it down – making a few helpful suggestions along the way, of course. The play was called 'Hamlet'. It turned out quite well in the end.

His stories weren't always original, though, I have to say. He wasn't worried where he got his inspiration. Like using Sycorax as the name of a witch after he heard me say it. 'All the world's a stage' – that was one of mine too.

Most of Shakespeare's work, and certainly his best-known plays and poems, date from the period between 1589 and 1613.

LITTLE IS KNOWN BY _YOU_, MAYBE.

For all his plays, however, little is known about the man himself. He married Anne Hathaway in 1582 and they had three children; Susanna was born soon after they married, with twins Judith and Hamnet born in 1585. Shakespeare's only son, Hamnet, died aged just eleven.

AND THE WORLD ALMOST DIED WITH HIM, OR SOON AFTER . . .

I met Shakespeare for the first time in 1596, when I took Martha to see one of his plays. It was soon after his son Hamnet's death. Even in grief, Shakespeare's words were so powerful they freed the Carrionites, and his grief meant they could twist his emotions to suit their needs. The Carrionites are a nasty lot, if you don't know them (and I guess you probably don't). Got banished by the Eternals to the Deep Darkness.

Anyway, three of them reckoned they could use Shakespeare's words to create a 'spell' that would release the other Carrionites from the Deep Darkness. It almost worked too, but we changed the ending of the play they were using – 'Love's Labour's Won', it was called. No copies survived, which is probably a good thing.

THE DECLINE OF THE ENGLISH NOBILITY

B Y THE MID-SEVENTEENTH CENTURY AD, the nobility of England were slowly beginning to lose their political power and influence. However, many of these lords and ladies remained prominent members of their local communities.

I met a few of this lot – the nobility, I mean. Lady Peinforte is the most memorable. Lived in Windsor – she was a real pillar of the community. Though it was a bit suspect how people she didn't like tended to end up dead.

In 1638 a rumour went round that a star had fallen from the sky into Lady Peinforte's garden, and then returned to the heavens again. Actually it was a piece of validium.

NASTY PIECE OF WORK, LADY PEINFORTE.

The validium that fell into her garden should never have left Gallifrey. Validium is a living metal and highly destructive. Lady Peinforte made it into a statue of herself — (yes, she was that vain).

I managed to shoot it off into space, but unfortunately it fell back to Earth in 1988 — which is where Lady Peinforte went. She had a mathematician work out when it would return, then killed him and used his blood as part of a 'spell' to travel through time to reclaim her statue. She wasn't the only one after it, though — there were also neo-Nazis, Cybermen, and me. It got quite crowded.

THE ENGLISH CIVIL WAR

WHO HAD ONE OF THE MOST RIDICULOUS LITTLE BEARDS I THINK I'VE EVER SEEN ON A KING.

THERE WAS CONSIDERABLE tension between King Charles I and Parliament for a long time before the English Civil War actually started. This culminated in King Charles sending soldiers to the House of Commons in an attempt to arrest five members of Parliament in January 1642. But the members had been warned of the danger and were no longer there.

When it began, the war was not a continuous series of battles, but rather sporadic, as were most wars of the period. In fact, there were only three major battles in the English Civil War: the battles of Edgehill in 1642, Marston Moor in 1644, and Naseby in 1645.

STILL A PRETTY UNPLEASANT TIME, THOUGH.

Not sure I've ever been to the Civil War. Maybe I have ...
it's so difficult to keep track of these things. I did go to a
re-enactment once. That was in Little Hodcombe, where there
was a battle in 1643; the negative emotions generated by the
fighting then had woken the Malus, a living war machine sent in
a probe from the planet Hakol. After that, the Malus stayed
dormant until 1984, when the villagers re-enacted the battle
and it tried to make them truly fight and kill each other.

When I stopped that from happening the Malus destroyed
itself - and the church where it was hidden. Which was a
pity, really. It was actually a very nice church.

THE AGE OF THE HIGHWAYMAN

WHY DID THEY WEAR MASKS?

I mean, unless you were going to be robbing your friends and family you weren't likely to be recognised. It's just being pretentious.

IT WOULD HAVE BEEN EVEN QUICKER BY TARDIS.

HIGHWAYMEN WERE ROBBERS who stole from travellers. In Britain, highwaymen were active from Elizabethan times right through until the early nineteenth century.

← MORE FAMOUS THAN THE KNIGHTMARE?

The most famous highwayman was Dick Turpin. The best-known story about Dick Turpin tells of his rapid 200-mile ride from London to York on his horse Black Bess – who died from exhaustion – in order to establish an alibi. This same story was also told about another highwayman called John Nevison.

HE DIDN'T DO IT EITHER

The Knightmare was a proper highwayman. Or rather highwaywoman because she was actually Ashildr, the Viking girl I brought back to life and who couldn't die. She was doing all the robbing just to keep herself from getting bored. Well, I know how that works. Not the robbing, but the boredom.

She did a lot to deal with the boredom, Ashildr. Disguised herself as a man and fought at the Battle of Agincourt, for example. Founded a leper colony. She was even a queen for a while.

Sam Swift the Quick, on the other hand, was just a bloke. Chatty and witty, I suppose. If you like that sort of thing.

And the Knightmare apparently had an accomplice called the Doctor.

STRANGE, EH?

THE PLAGUE AND THE GREAT FIRE OF LONDON

I REMEMBER IT WELL.

THE GREAT FIRE OF LONDON started in a baker's shop on Pudding Lane just after midnight on Sunday 2 September 1666. It raged for three days, destroying most of the medieval city of London.

WELL, IT STOPPED THE TERILEPTILS WIPING OUT THE HUMAN RACE. I'D SAY THAT WAS A GOOD THING TOO.

One good thing that did come of the fire was that it all but halted the spread of bubonic plague, commonly known as the Black Death, within the city. The plague was spread by fleas living on rats, and the fire destroyed the slums where the rats lived.

I guess I should take some of the blame, as it was my burning torch that started the fire. Not really my fault, though, as a Terileptil knocked it into some straw. (The Terileptils were a group of criminals who had escaped from the tinclavic mines on Raaga.)

But this book's right about one thing: the Great Fire did stop the plague. We threw the adapted bubonic-plague samples into the fire. Killed it all off. Killed the Terileptils too, but that was their own fault.

HERE'S WHAT HAPPENED IN SIMPLE TERMS.

CRIMINAL TERILEPTILS CRASH-LANDED ON EARTH.

TERILEPTILS DECIDED TO WIPE OUT THE HUMAN RACE AND TAKE OVER THE PLANET.

TERILEPTILS MODIFIED BUBONIC PLAGUE SO IT WAS MUCH MORE LETHAL.

DOCTOR TRACED TERILEPTILS TO BASE IN PUDDING LANE IN LONDON.

TERILEPTILS ATTACKED DOCTOR, WHO DROPPED BURNING TORCH IN STRAW.

FIRE STARTED.

TERILEPTILS' SOLITON GAS MACHINE EXPLODED.

THINGS JUST GOT WORSE FROM THERE, REALLY.

THE DISAPPEARANCE OF CAPTAIN AVERY

WHICH WOULD MAKE MORE SENSE IF YOU MENTIONED THAT HE USED THE ALIAS BENJAMIN BRIDGEMAN.

HENRY AVERY briefly served in the Royal Navy before becoming a pirate. Known as the Arch Pirate or the King of Pirates, and Long Ben to his crew, he enjoyed a short but prosperous career as a pirate from 1694 until 1696.

What happened to Avery after 1696 is unknown – he simply disappeared. It is suggested that he changed his name and lived quietly either in Britain or the tropics. He was one of the few pirate captains to evade capture and retire with his loot intact.

THAT'S PRETTY MUCH TRUE.

HE WENT A BIT FURTHER THAN THAT!

When I met him, Avery was having a bit of trouble with what he thought was a siren. This ethereal figure appeared whenever one of his crew was injured and whisked them away.

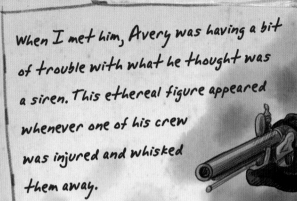

But she wasn't a siren at all. She was a holographic medical interface – like a sort of doctor – from a Skerth spaceship. She was taking away anyone on Avery's ship who was injured to cure them on the Skerth spaceship – including Avery's son, Toby, who had typhoid fever. But the cure only worked so long as they were on board the Skerth ship, so Avery stayed with his son, sailing through the stars. A bit different from the ocean, but I think he enjoyed it.

THE HUNT FOR AVERY'S TREASURE

HENRY AVERY'S capture of the Mughal ship the *Ganj-i-Sawai* has been hailed as piracy's greatest exploit. The East India Company estimated the goods on board the ship to be worth approximately $200 million in today's money, while others estimate the value as being closer to $400 million.

Some suggest that Avery was cheated out of his wealth when trying to sell diamonds to merchants in Bristol and that he died in poverty. But, whatever really happened to Avery, his treasure has never been found.

NOT STRICTLY TRUE.

Well he didn't take all of his treasure off into space.

'This is Deadman's secret key, Ringwood, Smallbeer, Gurney.'
That's what I was told by the churchwarden in a village
in Cornwall – just before he was murdered by pirates. The
rhyme was a clue to where Avery's treasure was hidden.
The names were members of Avery's crew and appeared
on tombstones in the crypt. And the flagstone at the
intersection of the names covered the treasure – which the
pirates forced me to tell them. Not that I hung around
to see how much was there. The revenue men turned up to
arrest the pirates, so I left them all to fight it out.

THE JACOBITE REBELLION AND BATTLE OF CULLODEN

'PITCHED BATTLE'. UNIT WOULD TELL YOU OTHERWISE – CYBERMEN, DALEKS, AXONS, SONTARANS . . .

DEPENDS WHAT YOU MEAN BY A

CULLODEN IN THE SCOTTISH HIGHLANDS was the site of the final battle of the Jacobite Rebellion that started in 1745. The Battle of Culloden was the last pitched battle to be fought on British soil.

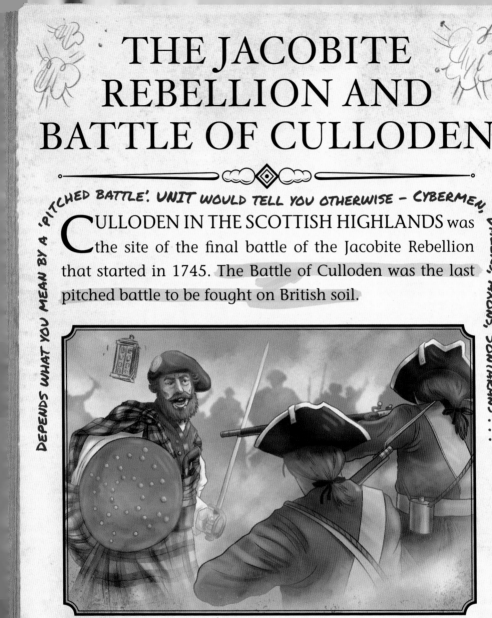

The battle was a decisive victory for the British government forces, and the rebellion subsequently collapsed. Charles Stuart, who had led the rebels, fled first to the Hebrides, pursued by the British, who put a reward of £30,000 (approximately £15 million in today's money) on his head. He eventually managed to escape to France, and never set foot in Scotland again. **PROBABLY A WISE MOVE.**

I have to confess that I missed the Battle of Culloden. Turned up too late, when it was pretty much all over.

It was still a dangerous time, though. I met some fleeing rebels and we got captured by the British Redcoats. They were going to ship us off to the West Indies and sell us as slaves. We managed to escape in the end, and we helped the defeated rebels we'd met to get safely to France.

All except one of them, that is. James Robert McCrimmon joined us in the TARDIS, and travelled with me for a long time - right up until the time Lords caught up with me, exiled me to Earth, and sent Jamie home.

LOUIS XV AND MADAME DE POMPADOUR

LOUIS XV OF FRANCE became king in 1715 at the age of five and reigned until his death in 1774. Most historians believe that Louis XV damaged France's power and discredited the monarchy; the French Revolution took place just fifteen years after his death.

WELL, HE DID GIVE AWAY THE AUSTRIAN NETHERLANDS AND NEW FRANCE IN AMERICA. WHICH WAS GENEROUS OF HIM.

IT WASN'T ME. HONEST.

The king's most famous mistress, and his confidante, was Madame de Pompadour. She was born Jeanne-Antoinette Poisson on 29 December 1721. At the age of nine, her mother took her to a fortune teller, who supposedly told the girl that one day she would become the mistress of a king. It was true – she met Louis XV at a masked ball in 1745, and soon became the king's mistress.

I did meet Louis XV. He seemed a nice enough chap, if a bit drippy. Met Madame de Pompadour (or Reinette, as she was known) a load of times, and she was much more interesting. Actress, artist, musician, dancer, courtesan. She was a fantastic gardener. (And a good kisser too.)

Though, I have to confess, I was a bit distracted by trying to stop a load of clockwork robots from killing her and taking her head. It was all a bit complicated, so I'm going to need some more space to explain. Sticky tape and paper to the rescue once again . . .

MADAME DE POMPADOUR AND THE CLOCKWORK ROBOTS

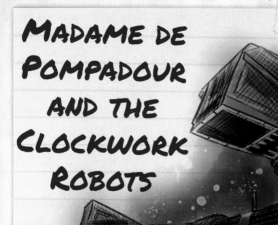

Well, it started when we arrived on a spaceship. Nothing too unusual about that, you might think. But this ship had a problem, and the repair robots were trying to fix it. They worked by clockwork, but they had clockwork brains too, which meant they thought that they could use bits of the crew as replacement parts. Which is rather unpleasant.

They'd opened time windows along Reinette's life because they wanted to match her age with the ship's age. More warped thinking - they reckoned that because the ship was called Madame de Pompadour they could use Reinette's brain to replace the ship's main computer. Well, no one said clockwork robots are clever, but as plans go, that is just plain bonkers.

I went through the time windows and got to meet Madame de Pompadour. She thought I was an angel, which is maybe a bit of an exaggeration. Anyway, I met her quite a few times in the end. The last time, I arrived through a mirror at Versailles. On a horse called Arthur. Right through the mirror. Very dramatic. Saved Reinette from the robots, sorted out the problem, then went back for her.

Except the time windows weren't very stable and sadly I arrived after she'd died. So young — even for a human. A great loss.

THE FRENCH REVOLUTION AND THE REIGN OF TERROR

THE FRENCH REVOLUTION began in France in 1789. Arguably one of the most important events in history, it created social and political upheaval inspired by liberal and radical ideals. The monarchy was overthrown, and a Republic was established, which ultimately led to the rise of Napoleon.

AND UNPLEASANT

I TOLD HIM AN ARMY MARCHES ON ITS STOMACH, AND HE GAVE ME A BOTTLE OF WINE.

With the execution of King Louis XVI in January 1793, the political landscape of France changed forever. Following the king's execution, the revolutionaries guillotined suspected enemies of the state in their thousands, during a period known as the Reign of Terror. *A GOOD NAME FOR IT. VERY APT.*

The French Revolution and the years afterwards used to be my favourite period of history. But that was because of the importance of the events – the events themselves were rather unpleasant.

I've not been to the revolution, but I was stuck in France for a bit during the Reign of Terror, just before Robespierre was executed in 1794. I ended up visiting Robespierre with a chap called James Stirling, who turned out to be an English spy.

It all got rather complicated and I had to break my friends Ian and Barbara and my granddaughter Susan out of prison before they got their heads chopped off.

THE INDUSTRIAL REVOLUTION

NOT THAT THIS IMPROVED EVERYONE'S LIVES. FACTORY WORK COULD BE TOUGH.

STARTING IN THE LATE eighteenth century, the Industrial Revolution saw a move from small-scale manufacturing often done in people's homes to large-scale factories, complete with specially built machinery that enabled mass production.

The invention of steam-powered machinery also led to the development of the railways. George Stephenson, born in 1781, was known as 'the father of the railway' because of his involvement in the design and manufacture of early steam locomotives. His son Robert was also heavily involved in the development of the railways.

HE WAS AN ENGINEER AND DID LOADS OF OTHER STUFF. DIDN'T BUILD HIS FIRST LOCOMOTIVE UNTIL 1814.

A formative and important time in human development. That's why both the Rani and the Master turned up when I visited the village of Killingworth during the early days of the Industrial Revolution.

The Rani was stealing a fluid from the brains of the workers that they needed to make them sleep; as a side effect, her victims ended up restless and violent. Not good. Stephenson, meanwhile, was planning on getting all the major thinkers of the time together. The Master wanted to use the meeting to push forward human progress. Not for your benefit, of course. It was so he could use your planet as a power base.

I managed to stop both the Rani and the Master, though they got away. But I sabotaged the Rani's TARDIS, so I don't think they got very far.

Life in Victorian London
THE WORKHOUSE

THE ORIGINS OF WORKHOUSES can be traced back to the Poor Relief Act in 1601, which created a national poor-law system for England and Wales.

By the nineteenth century, however, the old system of caring for the poor needed overhauling. In 1834 the Poor Law Amendment Act was passed, and meant that anyone without a job or home had to live in a workhouse. The theory was that by working for their accommodation people would learn to support themselves.

IT CERTAINLY DID. I'M SURPRISED IT TOOK PEOPLE SO LONG TO REALISE THAT.

AND, AS USUAL, THE THEORY GOES OUT OF THE WINDOW WHEN YOU PUDDING-BRAINED HUMANS GET HOLD OF IT.

Never had much to do with workhouses. Can't say I fancy the idea of visiting one. Certainly wouldn't want to live in one. Would you?

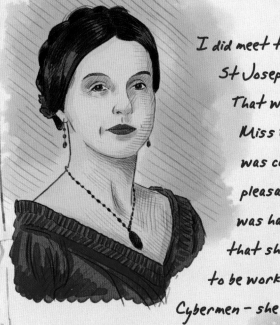

I did meet the matron of St Joseph's Workhouse. That was in 1851. Miss Hartigan, she was called. Not a very pleasant lady. Really, it was hardly a surprise that she turned out to be working for the Cybermen - she was supplying them with children from the workhouses, who the Cybermen then set to work generating the electricity needed to raise a huge CyberKing they had hidden under the River Thames.

The Cybermen betrayed her, of course. I could have told her that would happen.

As well as poor adults, the workhouses were also home to the sick and disabled, the elderly, and orphaned or abandoned children.

> PLEASE, SIR. I WANT SOME MORE.

CAN'T THINK WHY — THE FOOD WAS REVOLTING.

YOU CAN SAY THAT AGAIN.

The workhouses were deliberately designed to be unpleasant, to dissuade people from going to them for an easy life. The work was hard, the food was tasteless, and everyone had to wear a uniform. Children were often sent out to work in factories.

OR, AS I MENTIONED, TO CREATE POWER FOR A HUGE CYBERKING HIDDEN UNDER THE THAMES.

Thomas Barnardo had the right idea: he started setting up proper children's homes in 1867. He was a doctor, of course. Doctors always have the best ideas.

Speaking of doctors, I met another Doctor when I had to deal with the CyberKing. I thought he was another version of me – a later incarnation. I mean, he had a sonic screwdriver and a TARDIS and everything.

But his screwdriver was just an ordinary screwdriver, and his TARDIS turned out to be a hot-air balloon. His name was Jackson Lake, and he'd been brainwashed by an infostamp on which the Cybermen had stored all their information about me – so, for a while, he thought he was me. Nice chap. He was a big help, and he invited me to Christmas dinner too.

CHARLES DICKENS

CHARLES DICKENS is often said to be the greatest English novelist of the Victorian era. In addition to fifteen novels and five novellas, he wrote hundreds of short stories and articles. Well over a century since his death, Dickens's works remain incredibly popular the world over, and many of his books have never been out of print.

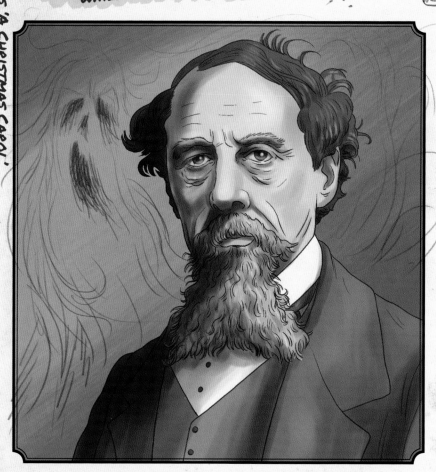

I only met Charles Dickens once, near the end of his life – though he didn't know that, of course. And I didn't tell him.

It was in Cardiff. I was aiming for Naples, so that was a disappointment. I was about ten years off as well, but that's hardly worth mentioning.

Dickens was in Cardiff to give a reading of 'A Christmas Carol'. It was Christmas, which I suppose was appropriate, only it didn't go quite as planned, because some real ghosts turned up. Well, not ghosts exactly, but an animated corpse. Pretty unsettling at the best of times, never mind in a crowded theatre...

HMM, THIS PROBABLY NEEDS A BIT MORE EXPLANATION. WHERE'S THAT STICKY TAPE?

CHARLES DICKENS AND THE GELTH

He was rather close-minded for a novelist, Dickens - sceptical about anything spiritualist or supernatural. So he got a bit of a shock when some walking corpses turned up. They were actually the Gelth - sort of ectoplasmic, ethereal wraith creatures - who had possessed and reanimated the dead bodies at a funeral parlour. A bit gruesome, but there you go. It takes all sorts.

They claimed they'd come from another dimension after losing their bodies in the Great Time War. But they lied about a lot of other things, so I'm not convinced that was true. They were planning to invade Earth, kill everyone and then possess the bodies of the dead. Not really an option.

So I blew them up, with a bit of help from a psychic lady called Gwyneth, who was possessed by the Gelth and gave her life to destroy them. Brave lady.

Charles Dickens believed in ghosts after that. A bit, anyway.

THE AMERICAN
WILD WEST

AS IF REAL LIFE ISN'T EXCITING. HONESTLY.

THE WILD WEST as it is depicted in films and other fiction is very different from the reality of the time. Life in the frontier towns that sprung up as European settlers spread across North America was not as exciting – or as violent – as is often portrayed.

BORING TEXTBOOK

Each town had a sheriff to keep the peace and enforce the law. Marshals were appointed at government level by the US Marshals Service. *I WAS A US MARSHAL ONCE. THOUGH MORE BY ACCIDENT THAN APPOINTMENT*

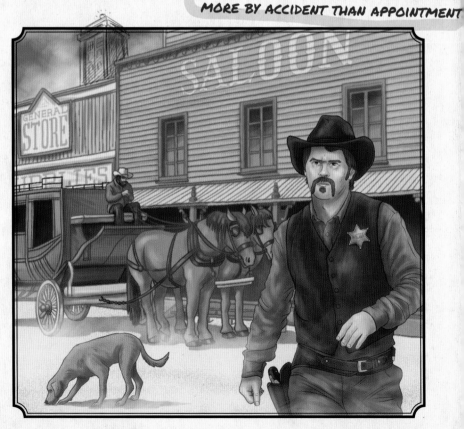

I became a US Marshal
in a town called Mercy
in Nevada. It was
about 1870 ...
I think. Maybe I
should have asked.
Didn't seem important
at the time - there
were bigger problems.
The marshal got shot
by an alien cyborg
killer, and when he died
he gave me his badge. So
I took over. Made Amy
and Rory deputies, and
off we went.

Well, we didn't go anywhere, actually - we stayed to
sort out the mess. It turned out to be quite a big
mess. A very messy big mess. There was this guy called
Kahler-Jex, who had arrived from space and given the
town electric lighting before it had even been invented.
He was being hunted by a cyborg gunslinger.

I'LL NEED MORE SPACE FOR THIS TOO.
SEE YOU ON THE NEXT PAGE ...

Right then, here we are. Kahler-Jex, scientist and doctor, turned lots of his own people into cyborg killers to fight in some war or other. A cyborg is someone who's been enhanced – so to speak – with electronic and mechanical bits and pieces. So it's like they're part way to becoming Cybermen. Not nice, basically. I wouldn't recommend it to anyone.

Anyway, one of these cyborg killers called Kahler-Tek wanted revenge for what had been done to him, which is hardly surprising. Ingenious lot, the Kahler – I quite like them, usually. Not so much when they're turning people into killing machines.

So Kahler-Jex fled to Earth and ended up in a Wild West town called Mercy, and Kahler-Tek came after him.

It sort of turned out all right in the end. Well, not for Kahler-Jex – he blew himself up to save the town. Difficult to be too sympathetic all the same, after what he'd done. Kahler-Tek – or the Gunslinger, as he came to be known – stayed on to protect Mercy. I guess he had nothing much else to do. He became the town's very own protecting angel. An angel who fell from the stars . . .

GUNFIGHT AT THE O.K. CORRAL

THE GUNFIGHT AT THE O.K. CORRAL became the most famous shoot-out in the history of the Wild West. It took place in the town of Tombstone, Arizona, on the afternoon of 26 October 1881. The gunfight was the culmination of a long-running feud between the Clanton family and their allies and the town's marshal, Virgil Earp, his brothers, Morgan and Wyatt, and their friends.

The gunfight lasted just thirty seconds.

I was there. Saw it all. Not pleasant, but then gunfights aren't really.

I was looking for a dentist – I had toothache after eating some sweets I'd got from the Celestial Toymaker (long story). Luckily – or so I thought – I found Doc Holliday. He had a huge model tooth hanging outside his clinic. A bit of a clue that it might be a good place to ask for help.

What he didn't have was much experience – I was his first patient. He didn't have any anaesthetic either – he did offer me whisky or a knock on the head with his six-shooter, though. I declined. I thought the toothache was preferable.

SO ANYWAY, YES. I WAS THERE. WITH TOOTHACHE.

THE MYSTERY OF THE *MARY CELESTE*

ULD BE INSULTED, WHOEVER SHE WAS. IF SHE EVER EXISTED. ACTUALLY, I DON'T THINK SHE DID . . . .

IN NOVEMBER 1872, the merchant ship *Mary Celeste* (sometimes wrongly referred to as the *Marie Celeste*) left New York for Genoa, but she never arrived. The ship was discovered a month later off the Azores Islands in the Atlantic Ocean.

NOT BY ME IT ISN'T. THE REAL MARY CELESTE WO

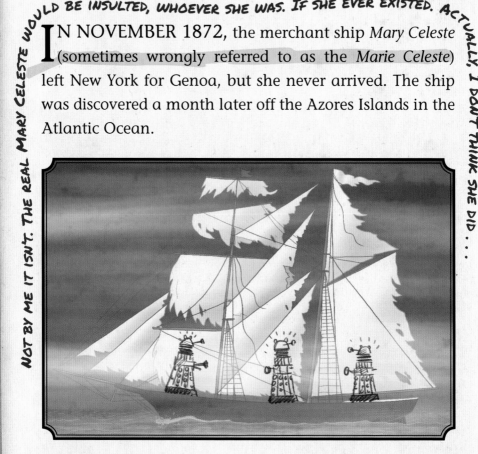

Although the *Mary Celeste* was seaworthy, there was no sign of the crew. The ship was well provisioned, and the captain and crew's belongings were still there.

What happened to those on board remains one of the most enduring mysteries of the sea.

NOT TO THOSE OF US WHO WERE THERE.

OK, I'll own up. It was my fault. Sort of. A bit. I suppose.

We were being chased by the Daleks, who had their own time-and-space machine. Not as good as the TARDIS, of course, but we had some narrow escapes — including on board the Mary Celeste. Here's what happened.

TARDIS LANDED ON MARY CELESTE.

DALEK TIME SHIP LANDED ON MARY CELESTE.

DALEKS DISEMBARKED AND SEARCHED SHIP, LOOKING FOR US.

CREW SAW DALEKS AND GOT FRIGHTENED. NOT SURPRISING, REALLY.

CREW JUMPED OVERBOARD TO AVOID DALEKS. A REASONABLE REACTION, THOUGH DROWNING'S PROBABLY NOT MUCH BETTER THAN BEING EXTERMINATED.

I DIDN'T WORK OUT WHAT WAS GOING ON UNTIL WE'D LEFT, AND BY THEN IT WAS TOO LATE FOR ME TO HELP. SO, MY FAULT.

SORT OF. A BIT.

QUEEN VICTORIA

VICTORIA NEVER GOT OVER IT. HE WAS A GOOD CHAP, ALBERT.

BORN IN 1819, Victoria became Queen of England in 1837, when she was just eighteen. In 1840, Queen Victoria married her cousin Prince Albert of Saxe-Coburg and Gotha. They had nine children together, who married into royal and noble families across Europe, before Albert died in 1861.

Victoria's reign spanned sixty-three years and saw great change. The British Empire was greatly expanded, and overall it was a period of industrialisation and scientific advancement.

AND SHE SET UP TORCHWOOD. THOUGH I SUPPOSE THIS HISTORY BOOK WOULDN'T KNOW ABOUT THAT.

She knighted me, Queen Victoria. About time too! Richard the Lionheart knighted my friend Ian Chesterton but not me. Queen Victoria also made Rose a dame. Sir Doctor of TARDIS and Dame Rose of the Powell Estate. Good, eh?

Not so good that she then banished us, though. She thought I was steeped in terror, blasphemy and death. Well, she may have been right, but that's hardly my fault. I don't go looking for trouble - not often, anyway. Generally, it comes looking for me.

Like the werewolf that attacked us. That's what Victoria was really cross about, though why she blamed me and Rose for it I don't know. We're the ones who saved her.

OK, SO HERE'S BASICALLY WHAT HAPPENED

1540: SOMETHING FELL TO EARTH AND LANDED CLOSE TO A MONASTERY IN SCOTLAND.

MAYBE IT WAS THE SPORE OF A VIRUS — WHO KNOWS? — BUT IT GREW AND ADAPTED AND EVOLVED . . .

. . . UNTIL IT COULD TAKE OVER A HUMAN HOST AND LIVE INSIDE THEM.

IT DREW OFF LOCAL FOLKLORE AND MAPPED ITSELF ON TO THE LEGEND OF THE WEREWOLF, TURNING INTO A HIDEOUS WOLF WHEN THE MOON WAS FULL.

1879: ROSE AND I MET QUEEN VICTORIA.

VICTORIA STAYED AT SIR ROBERT MACLEISH'S HOUSE, TORCHWOOD.

BUT SIR ROBERT'S WIFE WAS BEING HELD BY WARRIOR MONKS FROM THE MONASTERY.
THE MONKS PLANNED TO INFECT QUEEN VICTORIA WITH A BITE FROM A WEREWOLF SO SHE WOULD BECOME THE HOST.
LUCKILY, PRINCE ALBERT KNEW ALL ABOUT THE WEREWOLF. HE AND SIR ROBERT MACLEISH'S FATHER DEVISED A PLAN TO KILL IT – ALTHOUGH THEY NEVER GOT THE CHANCE.
I DID, THOUGH. I USED THE KOH-I-NOOR DIAMOND, WHICH ALBERT HAD CUT TO EXACTLY THE RIGHT SHAPE, AND A HUGE TELESCOPE MACLEISH HAD BUILT TO AMPLIFY THE LIGHT OF THE MOON.
DROWNED THE WEREWOLF IN MOONLIGHT. CLEVER, EH?

THE AGE OF RAILWAY

THE FIRST STEAM ENGINE – Locomotion No. 1 – ran on the Stockton and Darlington Railway, which was officially opened in 1825.

Before long, railways were the preferred method of long-distance travel. Trains offered speed and comfort that other transport could not. In 1883, when most travel was still uncomfortable and occasionally dangerous, the *Orient Express* began operating, and offered an unprecedented level of luxury and comfort.

NOT SURE I'VE BEEN ON THE ORIENT EXPRESS. NOT THE ONE THAT RUNS ON RAILS, ANYWAY.

RAILWAYS – I LOVE THEM.
STEAM TRAINS ARE THE BEST. OBVIOUSLY.

As a boy I always wanted to drive a steam train – as soon as I knew what a steam train was, that is. We didn't have them on Gallifrey. A shame. I think we missed out.

I may not have been on the Orient Express in Europe, but I've been on the other one – the one in space, in the future. That one travels between planets. Not that I had much time to enjoy it when Clara and I were on board. People kept dying, which rather got in the way of having a good time. More about that over the page . . .

The Foretold was a legend, a mythical creature that appeared to the people it was going to kill exactly sixty-six seconds before they died. Except, it wasn't just a legend; it was real. Here's roughly how it worked:

0 SECONDS: THE FORETOLD BRINGS ITS VICTIM INTO SAME TIME PHASE AS ITSELF.

10 SECONDS: PRETTY SOON THE VICTIM SEES THE FORETOLD.

15 SECONDS: IT DOESN'T TAKE THE VICTIM LONG TO REALISE SOMETHING'S WRONG.

20 SECONDS: OTHER PEOPLE SOON WORK OUT THERE'S SOMETHING WEIRD GOING ON.

30 SECONDS: IT'S GENERALLY ABOUT NOW THAT THE VICTIM REALISES NO ONE ELSE CAN SEE THE FORETOLD.

40 SECONDS: THE VICTIM REALISES THAT YOU CAN RUN BUT YOU CAN'T HIDE.

50 SECONDS: THE VICTIM IS SERIOUSLY FRIGHTENED BY NOW. TERRIFIED.

60 SECONDS: THEY'RE RUNNING OUT OF TIME . . .

66 SECONDS: THE VICTIM IS KILLED BY THE FORETOLD.

I saw the Foretold. But I didn't die – obviously, or I wouldn't be writing this.

I worked out that, while the Foretold looked like a rotting ancient Egyptian mummy, he was actually a soldier. All the technology implanted in him was keeping him going, and he thought he was still fighting his war. His camouflage systems made him invisible, and he only appeared to the people he was about to kill as he brought them into phase with himself.

Once I knew what was going on, it was easy enough to sort things out. I surrendered, and he thought the war was over and died. Which I suspect was as much of a relief to him as it was to me.

ACK THE RIPPER

ACK THE RIPPER is the name given to an unidentified serial killer generally believed to have een responsible for murdering and mutilating the odies of five women in London between August nd November 1888. Due to similarities seen n other murders of the time, it's believed hat he may also have killed others.

The fact that internal rgans were removed from everal victims has led to peculation that Jack he Ripper may have ad some medical nowledge.

The murders were ever solved, and obody knows why ack the Ripper topped killing.

PERHAPS SOME EOPLE DO . . .

THIS IS JUST A GUESS. YOU LOT HAVE NO IDEA WHAT HE REALLY LOOKED LIKE.

I've no idea who Jack the Ripper really was, I'm afraid. Maybe I should pop back and find out. Or I could ask Madame Vastra. I don't know if she got his name, but the reason the murders stopped was because she found him and ate him. Well, that's what she told me. Stringy but tasty, she said. I'll take her word for it.

There were rumours that Jack the Ripper had started work again a few years later. But that was Magnus Greel – a war criminal from the fifty-first century. He had to re-energise himself with organic distillations taken from young women. Not pleasant, as the process killed them. Killed Greel in the end as well.

VINCENT VAN GOGH

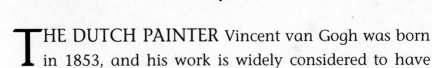

T HE DUTCH PAINTER Vincent van Gogh was born in 1853, and his work is widely considered to have had an extensive influence on twentieth-century art.

HE WAS CERTAINLY ONE OF THE GREATEST ARTISTS. AND GOOD COMPANY TOO.

Although van Gogh did not start painting until he was in his late twenties, he produced over 2,000 paintings, sketches and drawings in the last ten years of his life. He suffered from anxiety and depression, and in July 1890, at the age of thirty-seven, he committed suicide.

HE COULDN'T WORK WHEN HE WAS DEPRESSED – WHICH, OF COURSE, DEPRESSED HIM EVEN MORE. A TERRIBLE, TRAGIC THING.

When I met Vincent he seemed so full of life, even though he was nearing the end of it. But he thought he'd be forgotten and that his paintings would amount to nothing much at all. Amy and I took him to the Musée D'Orsay in Paris to show him an exhibition of his work so that he would see how wrong he was. I think he appreciated it. Amy hoped it would change him, break him out of his depression, but time and history don't work like that, I'm afraid.

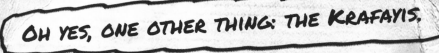

OH YES, ONE OTHER THING: THE KRAFAYIS.

There was a Krafayis loose in France, and only van Gogh could see it. He painted it into the window of The Church at Auvers – I had spotted it there, and that's why I went back to see Vincent. They're hunters, the Krafayis. And they're invisible to most of their victims. Van Gogh could see it simply because he saw the world a bit differently from most people. You can tell that from his paintings.

He was also ginger. Maybe that's why he and Amy got on so well. Two gingers. I've never been ginger. Some people have all the luck.

Anyway, the Krafayis killed a few people in the area before I got there. I had a plan to stun the creature with crosactic energy, and we cornered it inside the church. It was a good plan. Very clever. Very cunning. Except things didn't work out quite as expected, and Vincent ended up accidentally stabbing the thing with his easel.

GOOD MAN, VINCENT. GREAT ARTIST. A TRAGIC LOSS.

THE LATE VICTORIAN AGE

T HE LATE VICTORIAN period in Great Britain was dominated by two prime ministers: William Gladstone and Benjamin Disraeli.

THOUGH THE TERM 'PRIME MINISTER' WASN'T USED THEN. OR, IF IT WAS, IT WAS A BIT OF AN INSULT.

William Gladstone

Benjamin Disraeli

The British Empire was expanding and the prevailing feeling was that an expansion of British control around the globe was good for everyone. The Industrial Revolution had led to people migrating from the country to the towns and cities.

I'M SURE IT WAS GOOD FOR SOME PEOPLE. BUT NOT FOR EVERYONE.

I seem to have spent a lot of time in the late Victorian period. Not sure why, just the way things work out.

One of the times I ended up there, I met a version of Clara Oswald who was working in a tavern and as a governess. The Great Intelligence was just getting started and was bringing snowmen to life, creating people out of ice. That Clara died, poor thing. All the Claras seem to die...

I've made a lot of friends in the Victorian period too. Like Henry Gordon Jago, the owner of the Palace Theatre. And Professor George Litefoot, a pathologist. And of course Madame Vastra, Jenny and Strax – spent a lot of time with them. Hang on, I'll stick in another page...

THE PATERNOSTER GANG

Technically, they're not a gang as such, but I think of them as the Paternoster Gang because they live on Paternoster Row in London. Or they did, back in late Victorian times.

MADAME VASTRA is a Silurian – or Homo reptilia, if you prefer. She was woken from hibernation when they were digging the tunnels for the London Underground. She managed to fit in to human society quite well, though obviously she wore a veil most of the time. A green reptilian face does tend to attract attention – or so I'm told.

JENNY FLINT

is Vastra's maid.
They're also married.
Jenny's a nice girl, and
good in a fight. So just
step back and let her
get on with it.

And then there's
STRAX. He's a
Sontaran. He's also a
nurse – I know, weird.
It was a sort of penance.
Anyway, he's finished
the nursing bit now and
works as Madame Vastra's
manservant. Or Sontaran-
servant. Or something.

They're a good lot, the Paternoster Gang. They helped
me with the Great Intelligence, a nasty prehistoric
slug, a big dinosaur, homicidal clockwork robots, and
even some headless monks.

THE RISE OF THE 'MODEL VILLAGE'

← NOT A MINIATURE ONE, AS YOU MIGHT THINK.

'MODEL VILLAGE' was a term used in the Victorian era to mean an ideal community. Model villages were initially created in the eighteenth century by the landed gentry to provide good housing for the workers on their estates, and also to ensure that workers' cottages would no longer spoil views of the landscape.

YES, WELL, I BET THAT WAS THE MAIN REASON.

They could have given us a few examples of model villages — like Bournville, or Port Sunlight, or Blaise Hamlet.

Not surprised they didn't mention Sweetville, though. That didn't work out at all well. Sweetville was founded by Winifred Gillyflower in Yorkshire in 1893, and was supposed to be the perfect community. Mrs Gillyflower only wanted 'perfect' people to live in her perfect community. But no one who went there ever seemed to have any contact with anyone outside Sweetville ever again...

I went there. Got into a bit of trouble and had to be rescued by Clara and the Paternoster Gang. We found out what was really going on, and it was, er... too complicated to fit in this space. Never mind, I'll just stick over a couple more pages. You won't miss them.

Ah, that's better. Where had I got to? Oh, yes. We found out that Mrs Gillyflower had built Sweetville as a safe haven for her perfect people to survive the coming apocalypse. Trouble was, the apocalypse was coming because she was going to bring it about, along with her business partner, Mr Sweet.

Mr Sweet wasn't really a business partner so much as a parasitic prehistoric red leech creature thing clamped on to Mrs Gillyflower's chest. They'd built a rocket that would explode and spread poisonous venom from the red leech, killing everyone outside Sweetville. Then Mrs Gillyflower would be able to repopulate the world with her perfect people. I guess she thought it was a good idea. It wasn't.

She did actually launch her rocket, but Madame Vastra and Jenny Flint had taken out the poison, so no harm done - well, not as much as would have been.

THE FANG ROCK LIGHTHOUSE MYSTERY

YOU MEAN LIKE THE FACT THAT I WAS THERE FOR BOTH?

THE MYSTERY OF FANG ROCK is almost as notorious as that of the *Mary Celeste*, and there are distinct similarities.

Fang Rock is a tiny island off the south coast of England. In the early twentieth century, the only structure there was a lighthouse. One day the lighthouse crew disappeared. Evidence was found of a recently wrecked ship, which was thought to have belonged to Lord Palmerdale, but of the ship's crew and the three lighthouse keepers there was no sign.

IT DID BELONG TO LORD PALMERDALE.

128

I always hope that everybody lives. But sometimes, even when I do everything I can, everybody dies. Fang Rock was one of those 'everybody dies' situations.

And not just the lighthouse keepers. There was Lord Palmerdale and his secretary, Adelaide Lessage, and his friend Colonel Skinsale, and Harker, one of the crew of his wrecked ship.

The ship was wrecked in the fog because the lighthouse light wasn't working. And it wasn't working because a Rutan was draining the electrical power. Nasty lot, the Rutans. Like big green jellyfish with tentacles. Sworn enemies of the Sontarans, they can kill you with an electric shock – and they will.

The legend of the beast of Fang Rock provides one explanation for what happened. The legend tells of a hideous creature that emerged from the sea in the 1820s and killed two of the lighthouse keepers, driving the other one mad with fear.

A RUTAN IS CERTAINLY BLOBBY WITH TENTACLES, BUT IT ISN'T THAT BIG. AND IT'S GREEN.

Descriptions of the beast are varied and inconsistent. Stories of sea monsters have existed throughout history and, despite the lack of evidence, many choose to explain the mystery of Fang Rock as the work of such a creature.

THE RUTANS EVOLVED IN THE SEA, SO THEY AREN'T FAR OFF.

The beast was a Rutan scout, sent to make a survey of your planet. The Rutans were thinking of invading Earth, as it was in a strategically important position for their war with the Sontarans at the time. Which was going badly.

It took me a while to work out that it was a Rutan causing the trouble. It could change shape and imitate the lighthouse crew, which didn't make things easy. I eventually managed to kill it - but not before it killed everyone besides me and Leela.

Then we had to deal with the Rutan spaceship, which was full of lots more of the nasty, blobby, murderous green creatures. Fun day. We were heading for Brighton, which wouldn't have been half as dangerous.

BRITISH EDUCATION IN THE EARLY TWENTIETH CENTURY

IN THE LATE NINETEENTH CENTURY, public schools in England were regulated by the Public Schools Act of 1868. They were defined as schools that were open to anyone from anywhere in the country who paid the fees. *SO NOT JUST ANYONE — ONLY THOSE WITH MONEY.*

The 1902 Education Act overhauled the education system of England and Wales, establishing Local Education Authorities which funded the state-run schools and those affiliated to the Church of England and the Catholic Church.

MY CAREER IN EDUCATION

1913: History Teacher, Farringham School for Boys. I became a human called John Smith to hide from the Family of Blood. Happy times. But all things come to an end...

1963: I was nearly offered the caretaker's job at Coal Hill School, but the headmaster thought I was overqualified. He was working for the Daleks, though, so I wouldn't trust his judgement.

2007: Teacher, Deffry Vale School. I replaced a teacher who'd won the lottery. I posted the winning ticket through her door – I needed the job to deal with the Krillitanes.

2014: Caretaker, Coal Hill School. I got the job this time. But that was to sort out a Skovox Blitzer that was running loose.

WORLD WAR I

ALSO KNOWN AS THE GREAT WAR, World War I was one of the deadliest conflicts in history, and lasted from 1914 to 1918. It is estimated that nine million soldiers and seven million civilians were killed.

A SAD DAY. FRANZ AND SOPHIE WERE VERY MUCH IN LOVE.

The conflict was sparked by the assassination of the Austrian Archduke Franz Ferdinand and his wife, Sophie, in Bosnia on 28 June 1914. The complex arrangement of political and military alliances within Europe meant that, as a result of this relatively minor event, war became inevitable.

I once thought I'd arrived in World War I, but it turned out I hadn't. It was a war zone set up by aliens who had kidnapped and brainwashed soldiers from throughout your history. The aliens let the soldiers think they were still in the wars they had been fighting on Earth. Then the aliens were going to take the best soldiers and create a huge army to conquer the galaxy. Or something.

I realised there was something wrong when we wandered away from World War I and got chased by Roman soldiers.

I had to ask the Time Lords for help getting everyone home. That's when they exiled me to Earth. Oh, don't get me wrong — I love your planet. But I'd rather not be stuck here forever like you lot are...

BRITISH SOCIETY BETWEEN THE WARS

T HE PERIOD BETWEEN THE WORLD WARS, from 1918 to 1939, was one of upheaval and change in Britain. The coal, textile and ship-building industries were already in decline, and steam power was being replaced by electricity.

Having worked on the land and in factories during the war, women began to take a more prominent role in society and were finally given the vote in England. New leisure activities emerged with the arrival of the wireless, film and jazz.

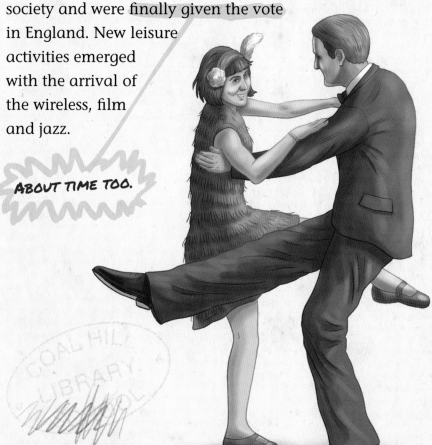

You lot tend to remember this period as all gloom and melancholy. The General Strike and the Wall Street Crash and the Depression and blah blah blah. But it wasn't all like that. Most people were better off. And there was cricket and dancing.

I played cricket with the Cranleighs some time in the 1920s. We also had a party and a dance. OK, there was a murder too, and a secret brother who'd been hidden away in the attic when he lost his mind and was horribly scarred while searching for the fabled black orchid.

It made for an interesting weekend. A bit like the time period really — some good things, and some not so good.

THE SS *BERNICE*

ON 2 JUNE 1926, the cargo ship SS *Bernice* set sail for Bombay. What happened after that is a mystery. While it seems that the ship did eventually arrive in Bombay, some accounts suggest it was never seen again.

NOT TO ME, IT ISN'T.

WHICH IS VERY NEARLY WHAT HAPPENED.

The reason for this confusion is unclear. Stranger still, there are reports of the ship making subsequent voyages, and Major Daly and his daughter Claire, who were passengers on the journey, are known to have spent time in India after 1926.

I think time has got confused. The SS Bernice did disappear without a trace, but then it didn't. Something like this.

SS BERNICE SET SAIL FOR BOMBAY.

SS BERNICE WAS TAKEN AWAY, SHRUNK AND PUT INSIDE A MINISCOPE (WHICH IS LIKE AN ENTERTAINMENT SYSTEM WHERE YOU CAN WATCH WHAT'S HAPPENING IN MINIATURISED ENVIRONMENTS THAT ACTUALLY EXIST INSIDE THE MACHINE).

MY TARDIS LANDED INSIDE THE MINISCOPE.

I ESCAPED FROM THE MINISCOPE AND POLITELY POINTED OUT THAT THEY ARE NOW ILLEGAL.

I SHUT DOWN THE MINISCOPE AND SENT ALL THE 'SPECIMENS' THAT WERE INSIDE IT HOME AGAIN.

SS BERNICE REAPPEARED WHERE IT HAD BEEN. SO IT NEVER VANISHED AT ALL – OR, AT LEAST, IT DID BUT THEN IT DIDN'T.

SIMPLE.

AGATHA CHRISTIE

AND THAT'S JUST ON YOUR PLANET. SHE'LL STILL BE READ IN THE YEAR 5 BILLION.

ACCORDING TO Guinness World Records, Agatha Christie is the bestselling novelist of all time; over two billion of her books have been sold to date. Although she also wrote several romantic novels (under the name Mary Westmacott), she is best known for her mystery novels, short stories and plays. She was born in England in Torquay, Devon, in 1890 and died in 1976 at the age of eighty-five.

OVER EIGHTY OF THEM. SHE WAS A MUCH QUICKER WRITER THAN SHAKESPEARE — IN HIS DEFENCE

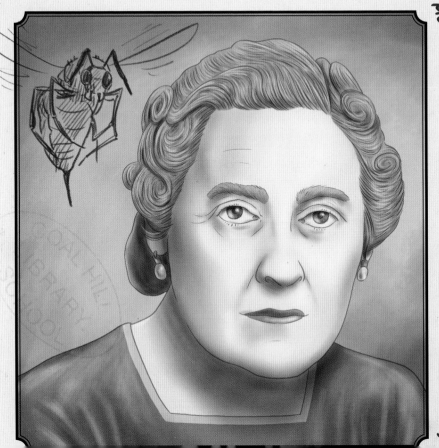

I met Agatha in 1926, at Eddison Manor. Nice couple, the Eddisons, though a bit old-fashioned. Well, it was 1926, so I suppose I should make allowances ...

Agatha went missing for ten days in that year. She was with me. Sort of. I dropped her off at a hotel in Harrogate ten days after leaving Eddison Manor. She lost her memory when a psychic link was broken between her and a Vespiform (like a giant alien wasp, though this particular one was disguised as a vicar).

It got a bit complicated. People died. But with Agatha's help I worked it all out. She was clever – a much better writer than she ever gave herself credit for.

THE WALL STREET CRASH AND ITS CONSEQUENCES

THE 1920s were a time of wealth and excess in the USA – until the Wall Street Crash. In October 1929, the United States' stock market suffered its worst crash in history. The Great Depression that followed lasted for the next ten years.

IT ENDED WITH THE SECOND WORLD WAR, THOUGH THAT WAS HARDLY AN IMPROVEMENT.

WANTED
A DECENT
JOB
FAMILY MAN
AGE 44

I was in New York soon after the Wall Street Crash. Not a happy time for most people. There were shanty towns all over America where homeless people went to live in makeshift houses and tents. The shanty towns were all nicknamed Hooverville after Herbert Hoover, who was the US President from 1929 to 1933.

There was even a shanty town in the middle of Central Park. A lot of good people ended up there, through no fault of their own. Some of them died when the place was attacked by the Daleks. But that gets a bit complicated, so I'll need more space . . .

DALEKS IN MANHATTAN!

Let's try to keep this simple...

The Cult of Skaro was a group of four special Daleks who hid in the void between universes until the Great Time War between the Daleks and the Time Lords was over. They even had names: Sec, Jast, Thay and Caan.

I thought I'd sorted them out at the Battle of Canary Wharf a few years ago (in your timeline), but they escaped to New York in 1930.

They had this crazy idea to mix Daleks and humans to create a new, improved Dalek race. So they made some people think they were Daleks, and turned others into Pig Slaves. Human pigs. Bizarre and sad.

Even worse was when their leader, Dalek Sec, combined itself with a human being and became half human, half Dalek.

They were based under the Empire State Building, which was being constructed at the time. It all got a bit messy.

Dalek Sec was destroyed by the other Daleks when he became too human. But then _they_ got destroyed by the humans who had been made to think they were Daleks, because deep down those people were still human.

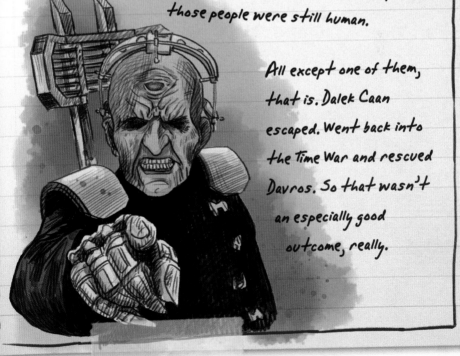

All except one of them, that is. Dalek Caan escaped. Went back into the Time War and rescued _Davros_. So that wasn't an especially good outcome, really.

THE RISE OF ADOLF HITLER

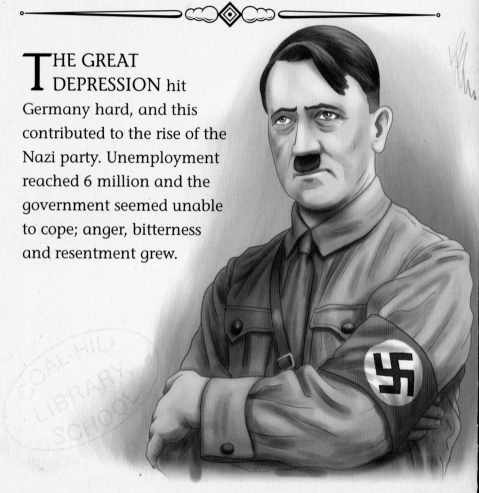

THE GREAT DEPRESSION hit Germany hard, and this contributed to the rise of the Nazi party. Unemployment reached 6 million and the government seemed unable to cope; anger, bitterness and resentment grew.

The leader of the Nazi party, Adolf Hitler, had been imprisoned after leading an attempt to seize power from the government in 1923. Just ten years later, in January 1933, Hitler was appointed Chancellor of Germany. He immediately set about making himself the absolute ruler of Germany.

THAT WAS THE HEAD OF THE GERMAN GOVERNMENT.

> I've met Hitler. Not a nice man.
> But I'm sure you know that.

I accidentally saved his life in 1938. The Justice Department had sent a Teselecta robot back through time to execute Hitler for his crimes. The TARDIS knocked the Teselecta over. Not a great landing — we came in through the window. But I was being held at gunpoint by a girl called Mels, who turned out to be River Song. Long story.

Anyway, Hitler shot Mels and she regenerated into River Song and tried to kill me. Rory punched Hitler and stuck him in a cupboard, which I think we can all agree was the best place for him.

LONDON IN THE BLITZ

PATERNOSTER ROW WAS DESTROYED THAT NIGHT. IT WAS THE CENTRE OF THE PUBLISHING INDUSTRY BY THEN, BUT I HAD FRIENDS LIVING THERE FIFTY YEARS EARLIER . . .

THE SUSTAINED AND STRATEGIC BOMBING of the United Kingdom by Nazi Germany, which became known as the Blitz, began on 7 September 1940 and did not end until 21 May 1941. The worst raid of London was on the night of Sunday 29 December 1940, when the German attack caused a firestorm that has been called the Second Great Fire of London.

The effects of the Blitz were devastating. Over 40,000 civilians were killed, and whole areas of London were decimated.

A terrible time, but the Blitz did bring people together. Hardened the spirit. At the same time, the German war machine was rolling across the map of Europe - country after country, falling like dominoes. It seemed like nothing could stop it. Nothing.

Then this tiny, damp little island says, 'No. Not here.' A mouse in front of a lion, I think was how I described it. When I was there during the Blitz, I told a girl called Nancy, 'You're amazing, the lot of you. Don't know what you do to Hitler, but you frighten the hell out of me.'

BUT THEN HITLER DIDN'T KNOW HOW IT WAS GOING TO END. AND I DID.

I was following a Chula spaceship that crashed in London during the Blitz. Turned out it wasn't an accident; it was a con by Captain Jack Harkness. Pretty typical of him. Except the Chula ship he'd used was a medical ship full of nanogenes — tiny particles that repair injured soldiers. Jack hadn't planned for that.

So these nanogenes found a boy who had been killed in an air raid and they repaired him. Except, being alien nanogenes, they didn't know what humans were like - they assumed his gas mask was actually part of him. So everyone else they repaired got a gas mask fused to their face too. The poor kid was frightened and only wanted to find his mummy.

Well, I found his mummy for him. Once I did, the nanogenes worked out they'd got it all a bit wrong and that his mum was what a human normally looked like. So they re-repaired everyone, and they did it properly this time. Off with the gas masks and back with the real faces. I like a happy ending. Or as happy as you can get in the middle of something like the Blitz...

CRACKING THE GERMAN CODES

VITAL TO THE ALLIED WAR EFFORT in World War II was the work of the Government Code and Cypher School at Bletchley Park in Buckinghamshire. Here, teams of code-breakers cracked the Enigma and Lorenz cyphers used by German forces to communicate.

THEY'VE BUILT MILTON KEYNES THERE NOW . . .

IT'S A WEIRD BUILDING, BLETCHLEY PARK. DISTINCTIVE, THOUGH. LOOK, HERE'S A PICTURE.

The Germans never realised that their codes had been broken. Some historians estimate that the work done at Bletchley Park shortened the war by as much as four years.

I visited another secret decoding centre – a military base in Northumberland. That's where Dr Judson had invented his Ultima Machine to decode German messages.

Unfortunately it was also where something else ended up: an elemental force of evil, born out of the creation of the universe itself. So it all got a bit hairy.

Decoding is fun, if you like solving problems, which seems to be what I spend most of my time doing. So I'm going to tell you the name of the elemental force of evil . . . in code. See if you can work it out. Ready? The name is:

6   5   14   18   9   3

ANSWER: FENRIC. So you figured out that each number corresponds to a letter of the alphabet, starting with 1 for the letter A, 2 for B, and so on in sequence right up to 26 for Z? Not bad for a human!

THE ROYAL AIR FORCE AND BOMBER COMMAND

T HE BOMBER FORCES of the Royal Air Force (RAF) in the United Kingdom were controlled by Bomber Command from 1936 up until 1968. From 1942, Bomber Command played a key role in the strategic bombing of Germany during World War II, working alongside the US Air Force.

However, bombing from high altitude tended to be inaccurate, and the effectiveness of the bomber forces was generally overestimated. ←

THOUGH THE BOMBING WAS STILL DEADLY AND HORRIFIC.

On Christmas Eve 1938, I fell out of a spaceship. True story. Luckily I was wearing a spacesuit. I fell all the way to Earth, and was rescued by a nice lady called Madge.

Three years later, Madge's husband, Reg – a bomber pilot – was lost on a raid, presumed dead. Madge took her children to Dorset for Christmas, and I became caretaker at their house so I could make it the best Christmas ever.

There was some trouble with a gateway to another world and an intelligent forest, though. Madge rescued a king and queen made of wood, piloting their ship into the time vortex for them by thinking of her home. And her husband, Reg – she thought about him too. Her love for him was so great that it drew his plane into the time vortex and led Reg and his aircraft back home. Which was a surprise. And probably the best Christmas present ever.

BRITISH SECRET WEAPONS OF WORLD WAR II

SOMETIMES IT'S A SHAME THAT THINGS CAN'T BE UN-INVENTED.

DURING WORLD WAR II, both sides developed ever more powerful weapons, with the most devastating being the atomic bomb, the invention of which changed the world forever. But defensive technology was also developed. Radar, or RDF (Radio Direction Finding), helped Britain to win the air war. Other projects remain secret even to this day. There is mention in declassified British files of the Ironside Project, for example, but nowhere is there any explanation of what this project entailed.

JUST AS WELL.

The clever thing was the way the British incorporated radar into their national air-defence systems. They also had great big microphones set up on the coast which could hear incoming planes. Crude, but clever. War is terrible, but good ideas come out of it as well as bad ones.

Now, the Ironsides – they were a very different proposition. They weren't really a British invention at all, though Churchill thought they were. They had him worried though, so I guess that's why he called me in. Turn the page and I'll explain . . .

THE IRONSIDE PROJECT

Professor Bracewell claimed to have developed the Ironsides. I think he really believed he had developed them, but I knew he was wrong. Bracewell was a robot, and the Ironsides were actually Daleks. Unsurprisingly, they made impressive weapons. That's pretty much what Daleks are, after all: a weaponised life form.

Anyway, the whole thing was a trap for me. The Daleks needed me there to say that they were Daleks. It wasn't just vanity – a Progenitor device they'd found left over from the Time War didn't recognise them for what they really were. But, with my testimony, the Progenitor accepted them as Daleks and created a new race of them – the New Dalek Paradigm.

I was lucky to get off the
Dalek spaceship in one piece.
I had a bit of help from a
jammy dodger, and from some
Spitfires that Bracewell had
modified so they could go into space.

THE DALEKS SURVIVED. AND THAT'S
THE TROUBLE, REALLY - THE
DALEKS ALWAYS SURVIVE.

THE CORONATION OF QUEEN ELIZABETH II

Q UEEN ELIZABETH II ACCEDED to the throne following the death of her father, King George VI, on 6 February 1952. Her coronation took place over a year later, on 2 June 1953 at Westminster Abbey. For the first time the ceremony – with the exception of the anointing and communion – was televised.

THE BIGGEST TELEVISION EVENT EVER AT THE TIME – WHICH WAS WHY THE WIRE AIMED TO EXPLOIT IT.

I missed seeing the coronation on telly, though nearly twenty million people in Britain watched it, apparently. Anyone with a television had a lot of visitors that day! I must pop back and see it.

I was a bit distracted when I was there. Rose had had her face stolen, and I was stuck halfway up the television transmitter tower at Alexandra Palace in Muswell Hill in London. Not somewhere I'd usually choose to be, I should tell you. But I was trying to stop an alien life form that fed on the electrical activity in people's brains.

Oh, there's no room here. Let me get the sticky tape again . . .

The alien life form was called the Wire, which is a bit unimaginative. It had been deprived of its real body – and maybe its imagination – by its own race. Whether it was as punishment for a crime or for some other reason, I don't know. The Wire never told me. Well, I never asked.

It came to Earth in a bolt of lightning, and it fed on the electrical activity in the human brain. By feeding on people's life forces, it planned to create a new body for itself. The problem was, everyone it fed on was left mindless and faceless – including my friend Rose Tyler.

But the Wire's main plan was to use television. It could exist in the electrical circuits, reaching out from TV sets for more victims. And, with Elizabeth II's coronation set to be the biggest television event so far in history, it just had to plug in to the TV transmitter at Alexandra Palace and it would be able to drain the life essence from the millions of people watching.

So that's why I was up on the transmitter tower – to stop the Wire. I trapped it on an old videotape. Well, I say old, but it hadn't actually been invented back then – it'll probably seem old to you, though. Having trapped it, I then erased the tape. Bye bye, Wire, and everyone got their faces back.

APOLLO II AND THE MOON LANDING

IN 1961 THE PRESIDENT of the United States, John F. Kennedy, pledged to put a man on the Moon by the end of the 1960s, and Apollo 11 fulfilled that promise. The Saturn V rocket blasted off from the Kennedy Space Center on 16 July 1969.

On 20 July, the Lunar Module landed on the Moon's surface. Six hours later, on 21 July, Neil Armstrong became the first human to walk on the Moon.

WELL, YOU COULD ARGUE THAT IT WAS ACTUALLY JAMIE McCRIMMON, AS HE CAME FROM THE EIGHTEENTH CENTURY.

I WAS THERE, THOUGH A LITTLE WHILE BEFORE THE LAUNCH.

I've been to the Moon a few times. It's eerily beautiful. And it's an egg. It'll hatch one day, but that's all a long way off yet...

I said Jamie was the first human on the Moon. I met him in 1746, so he was the human from the earliest point in history to walk on the Moon, but we were there in the late twentieth century (I think). When you're a time-traveller, things like 'first' get a bit confusing. Anyway, there was a Moon base that got attacked by the Cybermen and things became rather exciting and very dangerous.

The next time me and Jamie went to the Moon, we travelled in a rocket and ended up at a different moon base. That one was attacked by the Ice Warriors. Moon bases don't seem to have much luck.

A SILENT INVASION

I once met an impossible astronaut at Lake Silencio on the Plain of Sighs in Utah. It killed me - or rather, River Song did, because the astronaut was her. And, actually, it wasn't really me she killed either; it was a Teselecta robot ... It all gets a bit complicated and timey-wimey.

The Silence wanted me
dead. They're strange, the
Silence. They were originally
confessional priests. You
forget all about
them as soon
as you're not
looking at them and,
because of that, they've
been on Earth for ... well,
I'm not sure exactly how long,
but a very long time, and no
one's noticed. Or they have
noticed, but then they don't
remember it.

I sabotaged Apollo 11. Maybe 'sabotaged' is a bit strong,
actually. I inserted a video clip into the TV coverage of Neil
Armstrong stepping on to the Moon. It was a shot of a
Silent saying that you humans should kill them all on sight.
The post-hypnotic suggestion used by the Silence meant the
message was planted in the mind of everyone who saw it —
and just about everyone in history has seen footage of the
first Moon landing. Clever, eh? The Silence packed up and left
after that.

THE COLD WAR

THIS REALLY DOESN'T SHOW YOU HOW BAD IT COULD HAVE BEEN.

A LONG TIME FOR ANY SORT OF WAR, HOT OR COLD.

THE COLD WAR refers to a period of considerable political and military tension between the USA and its NATO (North Atlantic Treaty Organization) allies, and the Soviet Union and its Warsaw Pact allies. The exact dates are disputed, but 1947 to 1991 is the most commonly accepted time period.

There was never a full-scale war between the two opposing sides during the Cold War. Each side had a considerable nuclear arsenal, which served to deter the other from launching a nuclear attack out of fear of retaliation.

THINGS CAME CLOSE TO ALL-OUT WAR A FEW TIMES, THOUGH. IT GOT PRETTY HAIRY.

There was a lot going on behind the scenes to preserve the peace. When I was working at UNIT (the Unified Intelligence Taskforce – and yes, I had a job, though not really through choice), they were always off providing security for peace conferences.

The Master tried to sabotage one conference with a mind parasite that used people's worst fears to kill them. He was also after a nerve-gas missile to blow up the conference.

Another peace conference got attacked by an army of Daleks from the future trying to change history. It wasn't an easy time, the Cold War.

Oh, and in 1983 I got stuck on a Soviet submarine somewhere near the North Pole . . .

THE COLD WAR

Firebird was the name of the submarine I got stuck on - or whatever that is in Russian. I was actually heading for Las Vegas, so I'm not quite sure what went wrong there.

The submarine's crew thought they'd found a mammoth frozen in the polar ice. But, as they discovered when it thawed, it wasn't a mammoth. It was an Ice Warrior called Skaldak, and he wasn't very happy - partly because he'd been frozen so long he thought the rest of his race was dead, and partly because the submarine crew attacked him. He decided Earth had declared war and so he wanted to launch the submarine's nuclear missiles.

Ice Warriors turned up in a spaceship to rescue him.

The TARDIS, not being stupid, had left us and gone off
somewhere safer – it's the Hostile Action Displacement System
that does that, when I remember to set it. It moves the
TARDIS somewhere safer, but just a short distance away.
This particular time, though, I think maybe I set it wrong,
because the TARDIS moved from the North Pole to the South
Pole. That may be close in terms of the size of the universe as a
whole, but if you've got to walk then it isn't actually close at all.

rope

Africa

Asia

Oceania

ASIA, AFRICA, SOUTH AMERICA - WIPED
OUT BY THE DALEKS WHEN THEY INVADE
IN THE TWENTY-SECOND CENTURY.
ALTHOUGH THAT HASN'T HAPPENED YET,
SO I GUESS IT'S NOT REALLY HISTORY AS
FAR AS YOU'RE CONCERNED.

now I want to make sure it was worth the effort and that you were paying attention. So here are some quick questions for you.

I'll make it easier by giving you a choice of answers. No cheating, though. No sneaky turning back to check. I'll be watching (but you won't see me).

READY? RIGHT, HERE WE GO THEN. THE ANSWERS ARE OVER THE PAGE, FOR WHEN YOU'RE DONE.

1. WHAT WAS THE NAME OF THE JAGAROTH WHO GOT SPLINTERED IN TIME?
A. SEPHIROTH
B. KEVIN
C. SCAROTH

2. THE ANCIENT EGYPTIAN GODS WERE BASED ON WHAT ALIEN RACE?
A. THE OSIRANS
B. THE MIRE
C. THE ZOGS

3. WHO STARTED THE FIRE THAT BURNED DOWN ROME?
A. THE PYROVILES
B. EMPEROR NERO
C. THE TERRIBLE ZODIN

4. WHAT WAS THE NAME OF THE VIKING GIRL WHO I BROUGHT BACK FROM THE DEAD AND MADE IMMORTAL?
A. AGNES
B. ODINIR
C. ASHILDE

5. DID ROBIN HOOD REALLY EXIST?
A. YES
B. NO
C. MAYBE – I'M NOT WILLING TO COMMIT ONE WAY OR THE OTHER

6. WHO STARTED THE GREAT FIRE OF LONDON?
A. A BAKER IN PUDDING LANE
B. GIANT PLAGUE RATS
C. ME – BUT IT WASN'T MY FAULT

7. HOW DID THE ANCIENT AZTECS GET ENGAGED?
A. MAKING A CUP OF COCOA
B. BUYING A NICE, SPARKLY RING
C. DOING A SPECIAL DANCE

8. WHO PAINTED THE MONA LISA?
A. VINCENT VAN GOGH
B. LEONARDO DA VINCI
C. FLORENCE NIGHTINGALE

9. Why did I propose marriage to Queen Elizabeth I?

A. I really liked her

B. It was that or execution

C. I thought she was a Zygon

10. Who was the devilishly handsome accomplice of the highwayman known as the Knightmare?

A. Sam Swift the Quick

B. Dick Turpin

C. Me

11. Who was after Madame de Pompadour's head?

A. King Louis XV of France

B. Clockwork robots from the future

C. The local hat maker

12. Who unexpectedly turned up at a reading by Charles Dickens in Cardiff?

A. Walking corpses

B. The Prince of Wales

C. Lady Peinforte

13. Why was the Mary Celeste abandoned by her crew?

A. The cargo was leaking dangerous fumes

B. They all fancied a swim

C. They were frightened by Daleks

14. What creature did I save Queen Victoria from?

A. A vampire

B. A sort of werewolf

C. An enormous spider

15. Madame Vastra, Jenny Flint and Strax the Sontaran are collectively known as what?

A. The Three Billy Goats Gruff

B. The Kensington Set

C. The Paternoster Gang

16. What attacked the lighthouse on Fang Rock?

A. A Rutan

B. A Zygon

C. Cybermen

17. Did the SS Bernice vanish on its voyage to Bombay?

A. Yes

B. No

C. Yes and no

18. What animals did the Cult of Skaro turn people into during the Great Depression?

A. Pigs

B. Ducks

C. Geese

19. What were the Ironsides, which were apparently invented by Professor Bracewell?

A. Mini-submarines

B. Daleks

C. A new sort of chocolate biscuit

20. Which alien creature thawed out on board the Soviet submarine Firebird?

A. An Ice Warrior

B. A vampire from the Shades of Desparatis

C. The Vashta Nerada

THERE WAS AN INDEX HERE. BUT IT WASN'T MUCH USE REALLY. ESPECIALLY AS I'VE REMOVED A LOT OF THE THINGS IT WAS INDEXING. INSTEAD, HERE ARE THE ANSWERS TO THE QUESTIONS ON THE PREVIOUS PAGE.

1. C	8. B	15. C
2. A	9. C	16. A
3. B	10. C	17. C
4. C	11. B	18. A
5. A — SADLY	12. A	19. B
6. C	13. C	20. A
7. A	14. B	

I HOPE YOU FOUND ALL THIS INTERESTING! I THINK HISTORY IS ONE OF THE MOST FASCINATING SUBJECTS THERE IS. BUT THEN I SUPPOSE, IN A WAY, EVERYTHING IS HISTORY TO ME. YOU STILL MAKE A DISTINCTION BETWEEN PAST, PRESENT AND FUTURE; FOR ME, THEY'RE ALL MUDDLED UP.

AND THAT MAKES IT ALL _EVEN_ _MORE_ INTERESTING